Emily waited, hearing Keith's footsteps on stairs. The closer they came, the harder her heart beat and the more her stomach churned. *Dear God,* she prayed, *Help me to…* The door opened.

"Em," Keith smiled warmly. Then he squared his shoulders and adopted his severe voice. "You wanted something, Emily?"

"I want you." Shocked at her words, she clamped her hand over her mouth.

He laughed and drew her inside and without a word led her up a flight of stairs into a room that was a jumble of papers, stacks of clothing, and half-packed boxes and bags. He closed the door behind them and reached out with both hands, pulling her slowly toward him, devouring her with his eyes.

Dear Reader,

The Promise Romance® you are about to read is a special kind of romance written with you in mind. It combines the thrill of newfound romance and the inspiration of a shared faith. By combining the two, we offer you an alternative to promiscuity and superficial relationships. Now you can read a romantic novel—with the romance left intact.

Promise Romances® will introduce you to exciting places and to men and women very much involved in today's fast-paced world, yet searching for romance and love with commitment—for the fulfillment of love's promise. You will enjoy sharing their experiences. Most of all you will be uplifted by a romance that involves much more than physical attraction.

Welcome to the world of Promise Romance® — a special kind of place with a special kind of love.

Etta Wilson

Etta Wilson, Editor

Tuesday's Child

LouAnn Gaeddert

Promise Romances®

Thomas Nelson Publishers • Nashville • Camden • New York

"Monday's child is fair of face,
Tuesday's child is full of grace."

Published in Nashville, Tennessee, by Thomas Nelson, Inc. and distributed in Canada by Lawson Falle, Ltd., Cambridge, Ontario.

Portions of this novel first appeared in *Good Housekeeping*, copyright ©1984.

Scripture quotations are from the King James Version of the Bible.

Promise Romances and colophon are registered trademarks of Thomas Nelson, Inc.

Printed in the United States of America.

ISBN 0-8407-7375-7

Chapter One

Daffodils in the Boston Common nodded their heads as if ashamed of their pale yellow color. Lunchtime strollers breathed deeply, happily, glad to be released at last from the damp and chill of winter. Many of them stopped to admire the daffodils—until they spotted a deeper, more vibrant color.

A young woman sat huddled on a bench, her eyes staring downward so that all that was visible above her beige raincoat was a mass of radiant curls glowing red and gold in the sun. A man walked by humming, *Casey would waltz with the strawberry blond.*

So deep was her misery that she was unaware of her admirers. Another fruitless morning searching for a job. It had been three weeks since she had been asked to leave her job as receptionist for an accounting firm. "You are so decorative, Emily," the office manager had told her. "We had hoped you would overcome your shyness, learn to be more assertive. It hasn't worked out, has it?"

Her half of the apartment rent was due now, and her bank account was nearing zero. She'd have had to move anyway. Allison was getting married. She wanted her new husband for a roommate, not Emily. But where could she go? To the Y? To another town? To the bottom of the Charles River?

5

"Morbid!" she said to herself and got up and walked home. In the lobby she picked up the mail and climbed the three flights of stairs to the studio apartment. As usual, the mail was all for Allison, except for one flimsy envelope that she opened casually then read carefully:

Peter Darrow found dead today. Graveside service 2 p.m. Friday, St. Peter's Churchyard, Stonefield, Mass. Asked you be informed. Has left you house and property. Bring proof of identity. Will meet with executors my office after service. Glad to serve you. Wilbert Wilson, Attorney-at-Law.

Who was Peter Darrow? Friday? That was tomorrow. She looked at the address. Emily Stanoszek. Could there be another? Stonefield, Massachusetts? She looked it up in her atlas. It was a tiny dot near the New York and Connecticut borders.

It had to be a mistake. She'd never heard of anyone named Peter Darrow. Mr. Darrow? Dr. Darrow? Professor Darrow? Uncle Pete? She sat huddled on a straight-backed chair wondering what to do. Finally she went to seek advice where she had sought it before.

An hour later she was walking up the driveway to a colonial house in Wellesley. A black Labrador retriever ran from the back of the house, barking furiously.

"Hi there, Ebony," she called, bracing herself. The dog reared back on his hind legs, put his front paws on her shoulders and began to lick her face with wet affection. She hugged him hard and stroked the top of his head.

In the meantime a huge Persian cat approached and rubbed against her legs. She pushed the dog aside, picked up the cat, and walked on toward the house. A middle-aged man appeared at the door. Charles Moffat had been both her English professor and her employer.

"Emily," he said warmly. "How nice to see you. Come in. Did you come for your car?"

"Maybe....I really came for advice." She rummaged in her purse and pulled out the mailgram. "I received this today. Please tell me what to do."

He read quickly and then slowly. "Who is Peter Darrow?"

"I don't know. I don't believe I ever heard the name before."

"A friend of your grandparents' perhaps?"

"I've tried to think of every single person I ever met in their house, and I don't remember anyone named Darrow."

"A friend of your parents?"

"I don't know. I was six when they died. I don't remember their friends." She was silent for so long that Ebony decided the conversation was over and went to get a tattered sock, which he laid at Emily's feet. She ignored him, and the cat jumped into her lap.

Dr. Moffat read the message again.

Ebony picked up the sock and gave her another invitation to play. She responded and the dog tugged on one end of the sock while she shook the other. The game was interrupted by the sound of a bus and children running up the drive and into the kitchen.

"It's Emily!" Sam shouted.

"Emily!" Carol ran into her outstretched arms.

The professor greeted his children and then asked them to be quiet. "I think I'll phone this lawyer, if that's all right with you. Maybe I can find out something more."

Emily had lived with the Moffats for a year and a half. After her seemingly rich grandmother had died penniless, the professor and his wife had paid her expenses in exchange for child care. While he was trying to reach the lawyer, she prepared the mock-pizza snack the children loved.

"Gee, I wish you'd come back," little Sam sighed

when he had finished his snack. "An old crab comes in sometimes now. She's afraid of Ebony, she won't play games, and…" He leaned over and whispered in Emily's ear, "She has bad breath." Then he asked in a small, pleading voice, "Don't you want to live with us any more?"

"I'd rather be here with you than any place I can think of, but I'm supposed to be launching my career." Suddenly her face clouded over. "The truth is I've lost my job."

She nestled her face into the cat's soft fur to hide the tears floating behind her eyelids. When she regained control, she looked up to see Dr. Moffat standing in the doorway. He motioned for her to follow him into his study. As she seated herself opposite him, she remembered other times she had been summoned to his study to receive lectures about how she must discipline the children. Today was different.

"I'm sorry your job didn't work out," he said.

"Same old story," she mumbled. "The office manager said I didn't assert myself enough."

He nodded. "You are so lovely and bright and gentle. But gentleness is not a commodity much valued today. Now, Emily, I have talked with Wilbert Wilson, the lawyer. He sounds like a genial type."

The professor picked up a paper on which he had made notes. "Peter Darrow was eighty-seven years old. He was raised in Stonefield, built a house—a monstrosity, according to the lawyer—and then boarded it up and went to Alaska. That was in 1929. Five years ago he returned and moved into a few rooms at the back of the house, where he lived in seclusion. A year ago he came to the lawyer's office and said he wanted to put his affairs in order. The co-executors were called in. It's a strange will in that the co-executors are whoever is president of the local bank and whoever is minister of the Stonefield church. The bank president is the same person who was president a year ago, but there is a new young minister.

"At that time, Mr. Darrow gave fifty thousand dollars each to a home for Eskimo children and to Williams College. He also set up a trust fund for the education of a child who lives in Stonefield. He willed his house and land—about thirty acres—to you. There is also some money to cover taxes, fees, and the like, and you'll get whatever is left over. It won't be much. Wilson said the house is of no value and should be razed. He indicated that he could find a buyer for the land. With his will, Peter Darrow left instructions for the kind of burial he wanted. You were to be informed so you could attend the service if you wanted to. Last fall he phoned the lawyer and gave him your address in Boston."

"How did he know me—and where I live?"

"I asked, but the lawyer said he had no idea. Neither does the banker."

"How did he die?"

"A neighbor found him sitting in his chair in the kitchen in front of an open window. An autopsy was performed. He hadn't eaten for a long time. He'd been dead a couple of days."

"How horrible," Emily choked. "He gave away all that money, then starved to death. Couldn't something have been done?"

"There was plenty of food in the house, Emily. And a phone. And money." The professor paused. "Now my advice to you is go to Stonefield and claim your inheritance. The town is straight out the Massachusetts Turnpike to the New York border—should take about three hours." Dr. Moffat chuckled. "The way you drive it will take four hours. Attend the funeral. Talk with the lawyer and the executors. Get the lay of the land, then come back and decide what to do with the property."

Emily sat silently, twisting a curl with her forefinger. "Maybe I should just load up everything I own and move to Stonefield. Allison is getting married and is

9

anxious for me to move out of the apartment. I have no place to go. I might just as well live in my own house in Stonefield."

My own house. She liked those words. Dr. Moffat tried to dissuade her. She could live with them in Wellesley while she decided. The house in Stonefield had been boarded up for years.

"Peter Darrow lived there. He even left food."

Dr. Moffat sat shaking his head. "Do you need money?"

"Oh no, I have plenty," Emily lied. "And I have my gas credit card. I'll be fine." She hoped she sounded more positive than she felt. "Stonefield is in the Berkshire Hills, not far from Tanglewood. Lots of people go there in the summers. Maybe I can find a summer job."

Emily kissed the children, said good-by to the animals, and drove back to Boston.

Allison greeted her announcement with barely concealed glee, waiting less than a decent interval before phoning her fiancé to tell him the good news that Emily was moving out. They spent the evening dividing their shared belongings and packing.

The next morning when Allison's fiancé came to help load the car, he handed Emily an envelope. "Allison tells me that when you moved in you paid half of the security deposit and half of the advance rent," he said. "I want to reimburse you—a hundred dollars in cash and a check for the rest. Thanks, Emily."

The trunk was soon filled, then the back seat, then half of the front seat. The plants, stashed on top of everything else, made the little green car look like a greenhouse. The Boston fern tickled her neck and the violets partially blocked her view, nevertheless she was ready. She kissed Allison and drove off, feeling strangely lighthearted for someone bound for a funeral.

Once she was out of the city and on the turnpike,

she drove slowly in the right lane. She patted the purse beside her, grateful for the four hundred dollars. That would keep her going for some time. Emily tried to imagine her new home—a monstrosity—but Peter Darrow had lived there and so could she. *Who was Peter Darrow?*

She was reminded of Blanche in *A Streetcar Named Desire,* depending on the "kindness of strangers." Emily was like that. Grandma and Grandpa had been almost strangers when they had come to New Haven to take her home after her parents' accident. They hit an embankment coming home from a peace rally on their motorcycle and were both killed instantly. She still remembered the pain she had felt when her grandparents had thrown away all her overalls, jeans, and T-shirts. But when they had completely reoutfitted her in the kinds of pretty dresses they thought little girls should wear, they had meant to be kind. They had sent her to good schools and good camps. They had never known how lonely she felt, how apart from other girls.

Grandma, that soft Southern belle, had always depended on Grandpa to make decisions and provide for her slightest whim. After Grandpa's death, Grandma made no adjustment for her diminished income and, sure enough, someone had taken care of her. Her accountant, a dear old man, had simply added to her mortgage and supplied money himself. Grandma had gone on buying pretty clothes, fresh flowers twice a week all winter long, even the car Emily was driving now. It wasn't until Grandma's death that Emily discovered everything had been bought with borrowed money. The house, the silver, the furniture, even the clothes had to be sold.

The accountant had been kind, telling Emily the facts gently and putting Grandma's frivolity in the best possible light. "She was so lovely, we all wanted to make her happy."

There was no money to continue her education, but Dr. Moffat and his wife had given her a home. She had worked hard, but she could never repay them for their kindness.

Would there be kind strangers in Stonefield? "So what if there are?" she said aloud. "I will depend on myself. I will be assertive."

At the toll booth she asked the attendant how to get to Stonefield. He started to tell her, looked up from his coins, and left the booth to lean into her car and point the way on her map.

Then he stood back and grinned. "You always travel with plants? So you'll look like an orchid in a greenhouse?"

She smiled and drove on.

The Berkshire Hills, lavender in the distance, were shades of green in the foreground, pale budding leaves contrasting with the almost-black of the conifers. The two-lane highway rose and fell, twisted and turned.

A few scattered moths began to flutter their wings in the pit of Emily's stomach. The fern tickling her neck became a major irritation. She passed a deserted farmhouse, partially covered by flapping asbestos siding, the empty windows staring blankly at the road. Was her house like that? She shuddered. The next house was a yellow clapboard near-mansion surrounded by manicured lawns and tall trees. Her house was definitely not like that.

As she entered Stonefield she passed a gas station and a row of attached shops, a post office and a bank, then the town hall. Ahead was a church that looked as if it had stepped right from the pages of a book entitled *Scenes of Old New England,* complete with graceful spire and fence-enclosed graveyard at the side.

The moths in her stomach multiplied and fluttered around her heart as if it were a lightbulb on a summer night. Stonefield was a lovely village, but she was a

12

stranger. Where could she leave her car? Would its contents invite thieves?

The road divided at the church. She took the right branch that, according to the sign, led to New York state. She found a parking place across the street from the churchyard and combed out her windblown curls, pulling a navy blue beret over them. Then she very carefully locked her car. The moths had turned into stampeding elephants.

It was exactly two p.m. when she approached the church. A young minister in a black robe came out of the door of the church and descended the steps, followed by a fragile-looking young woman with a guitar hung around her neck. The young man smiled at her, and the woman motioned for Emily to follow them.

About thirty people, mostly quite old, had gathered beside the open grave. Where should she stand? She was hoping the young woman would direct her when a portly man in a pin-stripe suit approached her.

"Miss Stanoszek?" He beamed at her. "I'm glad you're here. I'm Wilbert Wilson." He led her to a position at the head of the grave.

Why couldn't she have hidden in the back?

The minister cleared his throat. "Before we begin, I want to say a word about this service. There has been, I hear, some criticism because we are not having a church funeral. Peter Darrow left instructions and we are doing our best to honor them." He nodded toward the plain wooden casket, so different from the ornate one that had held Grandma's last remains. "Let us begin. 'Let not your heart be troubled; ye believe in God, believe also in me....' "

Emily felt the moths fold their wings. She looked around her. Among the mourners was one child. Was he the boy for whom Mr. Darrow had set up a trust? Probably. He was standing between a middle-aged man and woman, both with the ruddy complexions of people who work outside.

13

Emily listened carefully as the minister prayed a prayer of thanks for Peter Darrow's life and reminded God that the old man had loved the little creatures of His kingdom, especially the beavers. That, thought Emily, was the first clue she had to the character of her unknown benefactor. He loved beavers.

"...loyal friend, fiercely independent...Into Thy hands we commend his spirit. Amen."

The young woman stepped forward, tuned her guitar briefly, played a chord, and then began to sing in a sweet, clear voice, "Amazing grace, how sweet the sound..." One of the elderly women added her cracked voice to the second verse and was joined by others. Emily joined in the last line. "A life of joy and peace."

The minister's simple benediction closed the service. "Peace I leave with you, my peace I give unto you; not as the world giveth, give I unto you. Let not your heart be troubled, neither let it be afraid."

There were tears in Emily's eyes for a man she had never met. The minister stepped back and six men lowered the simple box into the grave. Emily was about to turn away when the lawyer took her elbow and led her forward.

"Just pick up a handful of dirt and drop it on the casket," he whispered.

She? That should be done by his wife or daughter, a close friend. She was overcome by grief. This man had no one. She stepped forward and dropped the moist black soil into the grave.

As Wilbert Wilson was leading her toward the main street, an old woman shaped like a lumpy pillow stepped forward. She patted Emily's arm and looked inquiringly into her face. "We never knew about you," she said quietly. "Please accept our sympathy. Peter always liked pretty girls."

Although she wanted to cry out that she didn't

know this Peter Darrow, had never even heard his name until yesterday, she smiled and walked on beside the lawyer.

"...pretty little village," Mr. Wilson was saying. "Of course there's nothing here to amuse a city girl like you, but we'll try to make your brief stay as pleasant as possible. It's a simple will so I expect we'll be able to get it through probate without any difficulty. Then you can sell out. I'll take care of everything." He led her to a small clapboard building next to the post office. A brass plate informed her that it was his office.

They walked through the outer office, past a large middle-aged woman who did not look up from her typing. The lawyer's private office was opulent, with walls of shelves, rich paneling, and thick carpeting.

A stern-looking man rose from one of the leather chairs as they entered. "James Yost," he said, extending his hand.

Emily remembered him as one of the men who had helped lower the casket. He was tall and slim, with a pinched face, thinning white hair, and a mole on his jaw.

"Yost is president of the bank and executor of the estate."

"One of two executors," Mr. Yost said dryly. "Where's Calvin?"

"I didn't invite him. This is just a preliminary meeting. He's so young. I'm sure Peter Darrow had the old minister in mind when he wrote his will."

"We don't know what Peter Darrow had in mind. As the will stands, Calvin is a co-executor. He should be here."

Shrugging his shoulders, the lawyer seated Emily in a magnificent maroon leather chair big enough to hold two Emilies. Wilbert Wilson sat silently behind his polished desk for a moment, smoothing long strands of hair across the top of his bald head. Then he looked straight at her, picked up the only document on his desk, and began to read: "I, Peter Darrow of the town-ship of Stonefield, Commonwealth of Massachu-setts…last will and testament…give, devise, and be-queath all of my property, real and personal, owned by me at my death to Emily Stanoszek, daughter of the late—"

"Stop," interrupted the banker quietly. "Let her identify herself."

"Really, James, you bankers are too suspicious. She says she is Emily Stanoszek." The lawyer beamed at Emily. "Can you suspect this charming young lady of being an impostor?"

"I intend to do my job conscientiously." The banker glared at the lawyer over his half-glasses, then turned to Emily. "Your parents' names, please."

"Grace Ann and Michael Stanoszek. I have photo-stats of their marriage license and their death certifi-cates and my birth certificate here." Emily pulled a large envelope out of her bag and opened it with shak-ing hands.

"Can you tell me the names of your four grandpar-ents, including your grandmothers' maiden names?"

"You're badgering the young lady," the lawyer said with a sigh.

"My paternal grandparents died in Poland. I never saw them and I don't know Grandmother Stanoszek's maiden name. My father came to this country when he was twelve. I have his citizenship papers here too. My maternal grandparents were Thadeus and Grace Ann Potter. Her maiden name was Gresham. I have their marriage license and death certificates."

"Are you satisfied?" the lawyer asked the banker. "It tallies exactly with what Peter Darrow told us. There is no point in reading on. It boils down to this: the exec-utors will pay all funeral expenses, estate taxes, any outstanding debts—though I can't believe there are any—and the usual fees to them and me. Everything else will be yours."

16

"It may be indiscreet of me to say this," the banker said softly, "but there is very little money involved. He made several large donations last year and there isn't much cash left, a few thousand dollars only. Plus, of course, the house and about sixty acres of undeveloped land."

"More like thirty acres," corrected the lawyer.

"I beg your pardon," said the banker coldly. "I understood that he owned all of the land from the Gilbert farm to the other side of the beaver pond."

"You misunderstood. He owned the land from the Gilberts' to the lane in front of the house. But nevermind." The lawyer turned to Emily. "Monday the man from the State will be here, and we'll all go open the safe-deposit box. The deed will be there. I'll bring it back here and examine it on your behalf. Who knows what else may be in that box? Coins? Jewels? Whatever is there is yours so you may have inherited more than Yost thinks."

"There is no safe-deposit box." Mr. Yost's voice was perfectly even.

The lawyer flushed. "Of course there's a safe-deposit box. I asked Darrow to leave the deed with me but he refused."

"I suggested a box but he said he had a place for his papers that was safer than my bank." He turned to Emily. The corners of his thin lips turned slightly upward. "Old timers who suffered through the Depression still mistrust banks, you know. I suppose he built a safe into his house. You'll have to look for it because we need that deed." He turned to the lawyer. "You have the keys to the house?"

"I do. But Miss Stanoszek—may I call you Emily?" Emily nodded. "Emily won't want to stay there, not in that isolated monstrosity. She'll be more comfortable at the inn in Lenox."

"But I have everything I own in my car."

"So give her the keys," commanded the banker.

17

"She can store her belongings in the house and then stay at the inn if she chooses."

"I planned to stay in the house," Emily whispered.

"Good," James Yost said. "That's settled and I, for one, am relieved. I've been worried about Job and Bertha. The Gilberts say they tried to lure the dogs to their place but they wouldn't go. Tommy has been feeding them. Still they've been locked out of the house and the nights have been cold."

"Oh, for heaven's sake," groaned the lawyer. "I'll call the shelter and have them come for those mongrels. They're a nuisance, strolling down the middle of the road just daring some driver to hit them. I almost hit Job myself the other day. Would have if I hadn't swerved to the shoulder and been splattered with mud."

The banker turned to Emily. "Those dogs meant everything to Mr. Darrow during his last years—the dogs and the beavers. That's why I can't believe he sold the beaver pond."

"I can stay in the house and take care of the dogs. Perhaps Peter Darrow had that in mind."

"Highly irregular." Wilbert Wilson took a ring of keys from his drawer and handed them to Emily, warning her that most of the house was boarded up and that it was terribly isolated. The roof probably leaked and there were surely bats.

"Peter Darrow lived in that house for the past five years," Mr. Yost informed Emily. "I assume that the water has not been turned off, or the electricity, or the phone. I have to get back to the bank." He rose and took Emily's hand in his long bony one. "Phone me if I can be of any service."

When the banker was gone, the lawyer once again tried to dissuade Emily from staying in the house, reminding her of the bats and offering to take the dogs to the shelter. It was Emily's habit to respond to the kindness of strangers and Wilbert Wilson did appear

18

kind. Nevertheless she remained firm. She even refused his offer to drive her to the house.

"Be careful of the dogs," he warned. "They could be vicious, especially the male." He smiled at her. "Remember, I'm here to make things easy for you. If you have any problems or worries, just bring them to your old Uncle Will. I'll take care of you." He patted her shoulder.

"Do you know why he left the property to me?"

Wilson shook his head. "He probably had a youthful indiscretion. Maybe he cheated your grandfather and then escaped to Alaska and finally wanted to atone. Or maybe he had an affair with your grandmother and you are really his granddaughter. That's the story the local people prefer. Maybe he just saw you some place and liked your looks. He did say of you, 'she has a halo of gold.' " The lawyer ran his pudgy fingers through her hair. "I see what he meant."

Chapter Two

Emily stood on the sidewalk in front of the lawyer's office and examined the main street of Stonefield. On one side of the office was a red barn set back from the road with a brick patio in front—a closed restaurant. On the other side, beyond the post office and the town hall, was the bank. Across the street was a row of shops connected by a porch one step up from the sidewalk. The largest shop was the general store. A sign pointed up a paved street to "Lumber and Hardware."

Emily crossed to the general store. She couldn't believe that Peter Darrow's dogs were really fierce—the Moffats' Ebony looked vicious but he had the spirit of a mouse—still, a bribe wouldn't hurt. Inside, the general store was dim with small overhead bulbs, a wooden floor, and an incongruous stainless-steel meat counter.

"Ah, here comes Peter Darrow's heir," the grocer boomed from the back of the store as she entered. "Welcome to Stonefield. What can I do for you?"

"A pound of hamburger, please," Emily was perplexed that the stranger knew who she was. She picked up a loaf of bread, a stick of butter, a jar of peanut butter, and a quart of milk. "Do you know what kind of dog food Mr. Darrow bought?" she asked.

"Twenty-five-pound bags of dry. But you won't be needin' any."

"Has something happened to the dogs?"

"Nope. Saw 'em today. Two sad-looking creatures, Job and Bertha. Reason you won't need dog food is that I delivered a bag last week—when was it—Thursday—with Darrow's weekly order.... Want a bone? Might help you make friends with Job. He isn't going to be real cordial right at first."

"That's a good idea. Thank you."

"How do you like my store?" the grocer asked from behind the meat counter. "Riley—he owns the lumber yard—he's always telling me I should let him put in bright lights and tile on the floor. I'd like that but the fact is that the summer people think my store is quaint. You should see it in summer. I put sawdust on the floor." He laughed heartily as he wrapped a bone. "See that wood stove? It's not even connected to a chimney but the summer people don't know that. I put a barrel of crackers in front of it—regular boxed crackers at twice the price, and stale." He chuckled to himself as he thought of the tourists. "Prices are higher in the summer but not for the local people. Expect you're anxious to see your house. Real fine house. Hope you'll open it up. All those boarded up windows give me the creeps."

Emily thanked him and smiled to herself as she carried her grocery bag to her car.

The lawyer had told her to drive back on the road she had taken into town and look for a lane leading to the Gilbert farm. There it was. Beyond that would be woods. She slowed to a crawl as she drove down the bumpy, unfamiliar road and turned right into the next narrow lane. Dusky woods loomed on both sides. She drove on with a sense of deep foreboding until the woods stopped. Ahead and to the right, up a gentle slope, was her house—brown-shingled with boarded windows. A verandah wrapped around two sides of it.

Bays jutted out at the corners, one of them rising three storeys into a round tower with a roof like a witch's hat. Her house was pure Victorian corn—delightful Victorian corn.

Down the slope to the left was what had to be the beaver pond, with dead trees standing like naked soldiers in the center, high grass all around, and little islands of sticks and mud. It was forlorn and ugly.

The lane ended abruptly at the base of a huge tree just coming into leaf. She turned right into what remained of a gravel driveway and stopped in front of the garage, where she was greeted by a cacophony of barks and growls. A youngish dog, maybe part shepherd, rushed to the car, jumping up on the door. Her fawn-colored fur was covered with burrs.

Emily lowered the window halfway. "Hello, Bertha," she said softly. "I can see you need grooming. Are those burrs hurting you?"

Bertha continued to bark, her white-tipped tail wagging frantically. Behind her stood a massive dog with a huge head, his short legs planted firmly, his teeth bared. He had the sad folds and pushed-in face of a bulldog and the long silky ears of a basset. His short coat was mostly white with a brown spot on his back and another covering one eye and ear.

"That's a wonderfully fierce pose, Job, but you don't frighten me."

Emily opened the door, gave Bertha a gentle push, and started to get out. Job approached slowly, head down, growling deeply. His mean-dog pose was so convincing that she retreated, closing the door behind her.

Safely behind the steering wheel, she tried again. "I've come to take care of you, Job. That's what Mr. Darrow wanted me to do. I'm your friend. See, I've brought you a treat."

She opened her bag of groceries and took out the hamburger. Bertha stuck her head in the window and grabbed a walnut-sized ball of meat from Emily's hand. Emily threw another ball of meat out of the window toward Job. The dog ignored it, but Bertha ate it and then returned to the car for more.

Bertha licked her face and tried to scramble through the car window to the meat. Emily pushed her back and once again opened the car door, a ball of hamburger in her hand. "Sit," she said severely. Bertha sat and Emily gave her the hamburger, then reached back in the car for more.

With her hand outstretched she slowly approached Job. His teeth remained bared and he growled deeply. Still she walked toward him. Suddenly he snapped and ran toward her, forcing her retreat.

In the car she sat staring straight ahead, ignoring both dogs. It had been a long, emotional day. She was tired and hungry. *I guess I have no alternative but to try to find the inn in Lenox,* she thought, tears stinging the back of her eyes, her head throbbing. She turned the ignition key and started the motor. Instead of waiting to say good-by, Bertha pricked up her ears, barked, and ran off toward the back of the house.

"Why don't you follow her?" Emily suggested, but Job remained on duty.

"Where are you, Job?" a treble voice called. The same boy who had attended the funeral loped out of the woods and ran to the car. "He got you trapped?" the boy asked.

Without waiting for an answer, he patted the dog fondly, grabbed his collar, and pulled him toward the garage where he attached him to a long chain. A furious Job stood growling impotently at the end of the chain as Emily got out of the car and threw the bone to where he could reach it. Then she thanked the boy. She wished she could hug him.

"Job likes me. My name's Tommy Gilbert. We didn't know if you'd be here tonight or not so I came over to feed the dogs. Glad I did."

"I am too. My name is Emily Stanoszek."

She shook hands with the boy. While he went to the garage for the dogs' food, she unlocked the back door and stepped into a small hall with three doors opening off of it. All were closed. She opened the one to the right and found herself looking into a tiny bathroom with a tub made for a midget. She switched on the light. It was dirty but the faucets worked and the toilet flushed.

Next she opened the door directly opposite the outside door and looked into a small bedroom. The door to the left led to a large old-fashioned kitchen with a wood stove, a basket of wood, a table, and two chairs. A large chair with deep cushions sat in front of the window through which she could see the two dogs eating from one large bowl.

Tommy was leaning into her car and, as she watched, he straightened up with the Boston fern and a shopping bag and started toward the house. She ran to open the door for him. Together they unloaded the car until it was empty and the kitchen was filled.

"You look like a knight in shining armor to me," Emily said to Tommy as she locked up her car. "I'd have had to spend the night in a hotel if you hadn't come to my rescue. Thank you."

Tommy blushed. "That's okay. I better go home now; it's almost dark. Should I leave Job on the chain?"

She shook her head. "Just wait until I'm safely inside. Are the dogs usually out at night?"

"They stayed in with Mr. Darrow, but we opened the garage so they could go in there if they were cold."

It *was* getting cold. She ran toward the house shouting a final "thank you."

The overhead light in the kitchen revealed dirt and grime such as Emily had never seen before. *Poor old man,* she said to herself. Then she opened the other door in the kitchen and found herself in a butler's pantry with a wall of glass-doored cabinets. Beyond was a huge room with a bay window. Even in the semidarkness she could see that it was a lovely room, with paneling up to the chair rail and a chandelier. In the bay was one large chair and a telescope. No other furniture. *This is where Peter Darrow sat to watch his beavers,* she thought.

She pushed open a swinging door and tiptoed into an enormous marble-floored hall. It was nearly dark but she could make out a grand staircase rising opposite the large front door. She flicked the light switch; nothing happened.

Her heels clicked on the marble floor making the silence seem eerie. She was tempted to run back to the lighted kitchen. On the other hand, she wanted to see the rest of her gloomy house. Emily threw open the double doors to the right of the main entrance and could barely make out a fireplace in one corner of an eight-sided room, the parlor. Behind it, also off the main hall, was the library, with another fireplace and a window seat between empty bookshelves.

Any doubts she had about her house vanished. An eight-sided parlor and a library with a window seat. What more could anyone ask for? She vowed to have the windows bared as soon as possible.

She ran up the broad stairs. "Can you see me, Peter Darrow?" she asked aloud. "I don't know why you built this house and then left it to go to Alaska. It's a beautiful house. I don't know why you willed it to me. Whatever the reason, I thank you."

She threw open the doors in the upstairs hall. There were bedrooms over the library, the parlor, the dining room, and the kitchen. There were also two bathrooms and back stairs, but it was too dark to ascend them. The bright light in the kitchen welcomed her after the semidarkness of the rest of the house.

Hearing a scratch and a whine at the back door, Emily opened it a crack and Bertha slipped in. She found her bag of groceries and took out a slice of bread which she spread with butter. She poured herself a glass of milk. When she went to the refrigerator to store the rest of her food, she was overwhelmed by a sickly sour odor. She pushed her food inside and slammed the door. She was too tired to clean it out.

She was also cold. She shoved a piece of wood into the empty wood stove and then some newspapers. She lit them with a match from a jar sitting beside the sink. The paper flared brightly and went out. She put in more newspaper, lit it, and again the paper flared and went out. She tried a third time, and a fourth.

"Do you know how to build a fire?" she asked Bertha crossly. The big dog wagged her tail and nuzzled close to Emily. "You really are a useless creature. You don't guard like Job and you can't build a fire. What good are you?" Bertha wagged her tail happily.

From somewhere far away in the house there was a bang. Emily gasped.

"Nonsense," she said to Bertha. "We'll just go investigate."

She crept through the kitchen door to the butler's pantry and the diningroom. She peered out into the vast darkness of the hall. *Nothing,* she thought as she let the door swing back. She ran to the kitchen, dumped the clothing off one of the straight kitchen chairs and propped it under the pantry door handle. She locked the door to the back porch. Then she switched on the little radio beside the overstuffed chair in front of the window.

Anything, she thought, *would be better than silence punctuated by creaks and bangs.* The radio crackled and the precise notes of Bach filled the air. One more clue to Peter Darrow's personality. He kept his radio tuned to a classical music station.

On top of the refrigerator she had seen a brush. She used it to brush the burrs out of Bertha's long fur. At

27

last she went into the bedroom for the first time to see if there was a place in the closet for her clothes. The closet was jammed with Peter's clothing. Too tired to sort them, she threw the heavy blanket off the bed and found that the sheets had been removed. She straightened up to go look for her own sheets and found herself staring at a painting in an ornate gilt frame.

Her heart pounded. Too weak to stand, she lowered herself to the bed. It was a painting of herself walking down the grand staircase in this house in front of a stained-glass window. She was wearing a pink chiffon dress with an uneven hem and a low neckline. She'd never had a chiffon dress in her life, certainly not a dress with a hem that hung in points. But it was her hair, strawberry blond in deep waves rather than loose curls. It was her transparent skin with a tiny sprinkling of freckles across the nose. Her green eyes. Her wide mouth.

Bertha came and laid her head in Emily's lap. Emily laid her head on top of the dog's and began to cry. "I do *not* believe in reincarnation. I *do not.*" At last she began to hiccup. Still she and the dog did not move.

The radio crackled. She heard another sound, a creak on the back steps. Bertha ran to the door and began to bark. Emily's hands were clammy. Bile rose in her mouth. Slowly she struggled to her feet and went to stand beside Bertha, then she heard a whine and a scratch on the door.

Relieved, Emily unlocked the door and opened it for Job, who snarled at her and then ran straight to the upholstered chair, barking at the box that was lying in it. Emily put the box on the floor. Job hoisted his heavy body onto the cushion and lay down. Every wrinkle sagged. His brown ears drooped almost to the floor, and his small eyes were buttons of grief. She approached to comfort him but he lifted his head, bared his teeth, and growled.

She returned to the bedroom where she took the

picture off its hook and put it on the floor facing the wall. She made up the bed, washed her hot face in the dirty bathroom sink, put on her pajamas, and returned to the kitchen for the radio. Bertha followed her back to the bedroom.

Far off in the house something was banging. Job was whining. She turned up the volume on the radio and lay stiffly on the bed. At midnight the classical station stopped broadcasting, so she turned to a rock station. It went off at three, and Emily still was wide awake.

Emily awoke through a haze of pink chiffon, remembered her terror, and burrowed deeply into the bed. When at last she opened her eyes, she saw the sun was streaming through the very dirty window.

The dogs were waiting by the door. Bertha greeted her with a wag and a lick and then bounded out across the lawn to the woods. Job refused to look at her until he was on the porch. There he turned and growled briefly before lumbering down the steps after Bertha.

Still in her pajamas, she ran through the house. The sun, streaming in the bay window in the diningroom, revealed not only the beauty of the room, but also crumbling plaster in one corner and a stain in the parquet flooring. The marble hall was stippled with streaks of yellow and blue. There was a stained glass window above the landing just like the painting! It was boarded up so that only a little light could creep between the slats. She'd have to get those boards removed right away.

But why bother? She couldn't stay in this house that terrified her at night with frightening noises. So where would she go? She couldn't afford a hotel, but maybe she could find a simple room in a house in Stonefield. She'd have to stay nearby until the estate was settled and the property sold. Then maybe she'd go to San Francisco; she had always wanted to see that town. But what about Bertha and Job? For better or worse, they were her responsibility now.

As she was thinking about them, the dogs began to bark. A car stopped in the driveway and a masculine voice greeted them by name. Emily made a dash for the kitchen and began searching frantically for her robe.

"Hey, Peter. It's Keith, back with the springtime." The back door opened and a bearded man strode into the kitchen and stopped in mid-step. "Who are you? Where's Peter?" There was a note of concern in his voice.

Standing in the middle of the kitchen in her filmy pajamas, Emily finally spied a patch of striped seersucker. She tugged at it until the pile of clothing on top tumbled to the floor. Ignoring the intruder, she thrust her arms into the sleeves and knotted the belt tightly around her waist. Only then did she look up. The man named Keith was tall and broad. Sunshine from the dirty window caught flashes of red in his dark brown hair and full, neatly trimmed beard.

"I asked you two questions. *Who* are you? *Where* is Peter?"

"Mr. Darrow died." She picked up the teakettle and set it in the sink, turning on the tap. "He was found dead on Tuesday afternoon in that chair. He was buried yesterday. I don't know why you weren't told. Should you have been?"

He took a deep breath and then spoke slowly as if trying to explain a difficult concept to a child. "Peter was my friend. My name is Keith Cavanaugh. I'm mapping the beaver canals and writing a book. I set up camp here last summer with Peter's permission and I'm coming back to finish my research this summer. Your teakettle is running over." He picked up the teakettle, poured out some of the water, and put it on the electric stove. "Now, once again, who are you?"

"Emily Stanoszek."

"Why are you here? Looks like you're moving in."

"Mr. Darrow left the property to me in his will. I think he expected me to care for his dogs."

"Why? I never heard him mention you."

"I don't know."

"How could you *not* know?" His blue eyes flashed with annoyance.

"I never heard of Peter Darrow until the day before yesterday. You can believe that or not, as you choose." She turned to search through the cupboards.

"If you're looking for coffee and a mug, you'll find them to the left above the sink." He stared at her in a cooly appraising way that made Emily feel like an insect on a pin. "You look like a fluttery bird. Is that why Peter gave you his house? He was a sucker for helpless wildlife."

The teakettle began to whistle, giving voice to the tight strings that stretched her body. He switched off the heat and prepared a mug of coffee for her. "I came today to check with Peter about setting up camp when finals are over next week and to see if any of the beaver kits are out yet. To finish my research I need to camp by the pond all summer. I suppose I should ask your permission."

"I don't know who owns the beaver pond. The lawyer tells me that Mr. Darrow only owned the land down to the lane."

"Of course he owned the pond. People were always trying to get him to sell it. They wanted to clean it out so that the summer dudes would have a place to swim. He kept it for the beavers. He said it was their pond, but he paid their taxes for them. If you want to sell it, sell it to me. Now if you don't mind, I'm going out to check my campsite, then I'll leave I'll be back next weekend." He strode to the door, then stopped and turned back to face her.

"Will you be here? Can anyone as helpless as you survive here alone? Try, Miss Stanoszek, to last one week. When I get back, I'll take Job and Bertha and you'll be free to flutter off wherever you please." The door banged behind him as he whistled to the dogs.

Blast that male chauvinist! She'd show him who was helpless. She'd take care of the dogs and fix up the house and find the deed. If she owned the beaver pond, the first thing she would do would be evict Keith Cavanaugh.

Fired with determination, Emily dressed quickly in jeans, turtleneck, and sneakers, and searched for cleaning supplies. Grandma had taught her that ladies never soiled their hands so maids had always done all of her dirty work. Emily had known no domestic skills beyond sewing—Grandma thought that sewing was proper work for ladies—until she'd begun to work for the Moffats in Wellesley. How she admired Mrs. Moffat, who approached cleaning as a necessary evil to be done quickly and efficiently, according to a plan, each person doing his or her part. Emily was grateful now for that training.

She began in the bathroom. Under the grime, the paint was cracked and peeling. She had finished the ceiling and most of the walls and was about to tackle the white tile and porcelain when there was a knock on the door. Before she could dry her hands, the door opened and Tommy stood in the entry hall.

"Hi," he said cheerfully. "How'd you make out with Job? Where is he?"

"Both dogs went down to the beaver pond with a man who says he camped there last summer."

"The professor? The professor is here? Oh boy! I'll be back." Tommy was gone like a shot, his steps thudding down the drive.

She returned to her cleaning and had just finished and was admiring her work when she again heard running footsteps.

"Bye, Tommy, Job, Bertha," the hateful man called, gunning his motor. "See you next week."

She opened the door for Tommy, who asked if he could help her clean.

"Oh, I don't know. You must have..."

"I helped Mr. Darrow clean. Last fall I helped him sweep out the whole house. He said he wanted it to look nice when Emily got here. And now you're here. Just like I told Dad. He said maybe you were just in Mr. Darrow's imagination. Then yesterday you walked up to the grave and I said, 'Look, Dad, there's Emily,' and he said, 'You're right, son, that must be Emily.' My mom got all teary. Before I forget, my mom wants you to come to dinner after church tomorrow. You don't have to come to church, she says, you can just come for dinner about one o'clock."

"Tell your mother I'll be in church—is it at eleven?—and I'd love to come to dinner."

"I'm really a good worker," Tommy announced. "It's too early to mow lawns and plant gardens, so I'll charge you winter rates. After the summer people come my rates go up."

Emily laughed and asked Tommy to begin by showing her how to get the stove started. He peered into the stove.

"What'd you use?"

"Paper."

"And this one log?"

Emily nodded.

"You can't start a fire with just one log. You need kindling." He removed the log, put in twists of newspaper and then strips which he broke from a shingle. Finally he added two logs and another on top. "When you want a fire, just light the paper. I positively guarantee it'll burn."

Having taken her instructions, she began giving them. They emptied the bedroom closet of Peter's clothes, going carefully through each pocket, finding nothing more interesting than a few crumbs of pipe tobacco and some loose change, which Emily insisted on giving to Tommy. They took the old coat that Tommy said was the one Mr. Darrow wore every day and put it on the back porch. Job came and lay on it. It was the first time Emily had seen him look contented.

Some of the clothes they put in her car to go to the Goodwill box in the village. The rest she put in plastic trash bags for the garbage man to pick up.

When they stopped for lunch, the grime had been removed, revealing a white ceiling, soft yellow walls with only a few cracks, a warm, almost new maple dresser and matching night stand. The room was flooded with light from the sparkling window. She'd used a cleans-as-it-waxes product on the floor and discovered that it was beautiful.

"Mr. Darrow wanted to clean up the floors after we swept them," Tommy explained. "He bought this stuff to do it with, but he wasn't strong enough. He was real old. I came almost every day this winter to get wood in for him. Sometimes he talked about Eskimos going out on the ice floe to die. Do you know that when Eskimos get too old to work they just walk away and die? Do you think that's what Mr. Darrow did? Do you think he just sat down in his chair and let himself die? I was here Saturday. The fire had gone out and he wouldn't let me build another. He told me not to come back. I told my dad and he said, 'let him be,' and then Tuesday he came and Mr. Darrow was sitting here dead and the window was open. I should have come back anyway, don't you think?"

"You did what he asked you to do, Tommy," Emily said gently. "Come see the bathroom. Doesn't it look nice? I think I'll paint it next week." Emily was shocked at her own audacity. She'd never painted anything in her life.

After lunch Emily stored the frightening picture of herself in the back of the closet. She put her things away in the bedroom while Tommy cleaned out the refrigerator. Among Emily's things were the ice-cream-plaid bedspread and drapes she'd used in her dormitory room. She covered the bed and asked Tommy where to get a curtain rod.

They had hardly begun on the kitchen, but at least the mold had been scrubbed out of the refrigerator and she could stock it anew She paid Tommy and asked him to come again the following Saturday. He was, as he had promised, a good worker. He was also a cheerful companion, unlike the man who had barged in on her earlier.

After Tommy left, Emily surveyed the outside of her house. There were two sets of stairs to the verandah, both badly rotted. Between the stairs were straggly bushes and one blooming crocus which delighted her. She walked away from the house and tried to imagine it without boarded windows. The brown shingles seemed to be in good shape, but what did she know about such things? And what about the roof? There were stains in the diningroom ceiling. Did that mean it leaked? Why didn't the lights turn on in the parlor and hall? She'd have to find someone who knew something about home repair to advise her.

She walked all around the house. Here and there were huge trees; one very close to the house. Could the frightful banging she'd heard the night before have been a branch knocking against the boards on an upstairs window? In the afternoon sunshine she was able to laugh at her terror.

Emily showered in her clean tub, dressed in a denim skirt, shirt and lavender sweater and drove off toward the village. Her first stop was the Goodwill bin, where she deposited Peter Darrow's clothes. Next she went inside the hardware store to buy a curtain rod. She had selected one she thought would be the right size when a wiry young man pushed a shock a blond hair out of his eyes, grinned, and asked if he could be of service.

"I need some paint," she said.

"What kind?" What did he mean, what kind? Was

there more than one kind? She shook her head and shrugged her shoulders. "What are you going to paint?" he asked patiently.

"A bathroom."

"The little one on the first floor?" he asked. "Ever painted anything before?" Puzzled that he knew who she was and knew about her bathroom, she shook her head no. "That paint is peeling badly, as I recall. You'll have to scrape it. Mr. Darrow probably had a scraper someplace. It looks like this." He held up a tool that looked like a spatula. "You'll need a primer." He took down a paint can. "What color?"

"Yellow."

He handed her a color chart and went to wait on another customer. She picked the shade of yellow she wanted and then walked around the store. Such a lot to learn, but she was determined. On a rack of paperback books she spotted one entitled *Beginner's Guide to Easy Home Maintenance.* Just what she needed! She eagerly took a copy off the shelf and flipped through it as she walked about the store. A display of metal shelving caught her eye. "Is this expensive?" she asked the young man when he returned.

"How big a unit do you need?"

"About this big." She indicated the dimensions with her hands. "In white."

Emily was pleased when he told her it would cost about fifteen dollars. It would be perfect under the window for her plants and books. But she was dismayed when the young man produced a small flat box. She'd have to assemble it, he explained. Emily was determined not to let her face reveal the sinking feeling she had in her stomach. She showed him the color she had chosen for the bathroom.

"You'll want enamel in the bathroom. High gloss, semi, or flat?" What language did this fellow speak? She stared at him. "Do you want it real shiny, a little shiny, or not shiny at all?"

"I'm sorry," she giggled. "I really don't know anything about this. I guess I want it a little shiny. I'm hoping this book will tell me what I need to know."

He laughed with her and began piling strange objects on the counter. She recognized the brush. "Anything else?" he asked.

"I want to hang a plant from the ceiling. What do I need?"

He reached into a box without even looking and produced a large hook. "Know anything about molly plugs?"

"Molly who?"

He leaned forward, his hands on the counter between them, and looked straight into her eyes. "I think, Miss Emily, that you have bitten off more than you can chew."

"How do you know my name?" she asked, bewildered.

"Everyone in town knows your name. We just can't pronounce your last name. So Miss Emily it is. My name's Eddy Riley. Now suppose I come out to your place when we close. I'll put up the rod and the hook and put the shelves together."

"Oh, but..." She must learn not to depend on the kindness of strangers. She must learn to do things for herself. She...

"I'll be there," he said, handing her the change and one package while he walked beside her to the car with the others. "You can offer me a cup of coffee if you think you have to pay me." His boyish grin reminded her of Tommy.

She made her other stops in town as quickly as possible and rushed home to feed the dogs. She'd seen tools in one of the pantry drawers when she was looking for cleaning supplies, and she was determined to get that curtain rod up by herself.

Emily had struck her thumb for the third time when

the young man from the hardware store drove into the driveway. The dogs greeted him with enthusiasm, following him into the house. He examined the rod which was hanging by one bent nail and turned quickly to see her trying to suck the sting out of her thumb. Without a word, Eddy took the hammer from her and climbed the ladder. Bang. Bang. Bang. The rod was firmly in place. He came down, picked up the drapes lying on the bed, and hung them.

"Nice," he said, standing back to admire his handiwork and looking around him. "Very nice."

Without another word he began installing the hook. She brought him a mug of coffee and went back to the kitchen for her Boston fern. When it was hung, he sat down on the floor and began to assemble the shelves. Emily was shocked at the number of little pieces that had come out of the box with the shelves, and relieved she did not have to try to put them together herself. When the violets were in place on the assembled shelves, she refilled his mug and invited him to share her supper—bacon, eggs, and salad.

Over dinner Eddy supplied more pieces of the Peter Darrow puzzle. The man's father had owned the lumberyard. Peter went to Williams College for a couple of years and then joined the army during World War I. By the time he returned from Europe, his father was dead, so he took over the lumberyard. In 1928 Darrow built this house on land he had inherited. Nobody in town could figure out why he built it; he was a bachelor.

Peter's boyhood friend, Edward Riley, worked for him at the lumberyard. One day late in the summer of 1929 Peter handed Edward a set of keys and said he was leaving for Alaska. He wanted his friend to run the lumberyard and told him he could have all the profits. All Peter asked was that Edward board up the windows on his new house and keep an eye on it. Then the Depression came along.

When things began to get better, Edward Riley went

to a lawyer who was known to be in touch with Peter and said he wanted to buy the lumberyard. Some time later he received a letter from Alaska saying the price was one dollar, which he could pay in installments. That was Peter's idea of a joke. He also asked his friend to continue to keep an eye on the house and make whatever repairs might be necessary to preserve it. Through the years Edward Riley, then his son, Ed Riley, and his grandson, Eddy Riley—the young man who was telling the tale—had done just that.

"Did you notice the stains in the diningroom?" Eddy asked. "We lost some shingles on the roof of the tower during a tornado while I was still in elementary school. Before we could get out here, water had poured down through the tower room and the bedroom above and into the diningroom. We put a new roof on the tower. After Mr. Darrow came home we wanted to fix it up. After all, he *gave* us our family business. We would have made the whole house ship-shape, but he didn't want to be bothered. He was just too old to cope. That's why the verandah is partially rotted."

"But you could tell me what needs to be done if I'm to stay here?"

"You plan to stay?" Eddy's eyebrows shot up in surprise.

"At least through the summer," Emily announced and found that she meant it. She'd outlast that Keith Cavanaugh whatever it cost.

Eddy said that his father was the expert and he would phone and make an appointment to survey the house during the following week. He thanked Emily for supper and was on his way to the door when he stopped.

"Tell me, Emily, are you afraid to stay here by yourself?"

"Of course not," she lied. "I have Job and Bertha." Then she laughed. "That's not exactly true." She told

39

him about the banging. They stopped to listen. "There it is. Funny I haven't noticed it all the time you've been here."

"I'll check and let you know." In a few minutes he was back. "It's the tree on the east side. The wind blows a branch against the boards on one of the upstairs windows. If you decide to remove the boards we could probably just cut the branch from the open window."

That night Emily went happily to her cheerful room, drew the drapes, and slept soundly with Bertha on the floor beside her and Job curled up in his master's chair.

Chapter Three

Emily slipped into a back pew just as the minister rose to give the call-to-worship. He was a very young man; this was probably his first pastorate. The young woman who had played the guitar at the graveside was playing the small electric organ in the church. It was a simple service of old hymns, familiar Scriptures, and a sermon delivered in a conversational tone.

She could already identify some of the members of the small congregation. There was the lawyer, Wilbert Wilson, toward the front on one side, the banker, James Yost, on the other. Tommy Gilbert sat in the pew in front of her with his parents and the lumpy-pillow woman who had spoken to Emily after the funeral.

With the last strains of "God Be with You till We Meet Again," Emily felt a familiar surge of shyness. She stood, hesitating, in the pew.

"How nice to see you here!" Tommy's mother turned, her hand extended. "I'm Ruth Gilbert and this is my mother-in-law, Hilda Gilbert." Each of the Gilbert women shook Emily's hand. "Did you drive? I'd like to hurry home to check the roast. I'd appreciate it if you'd bring Mom and her friend with you."

Emily said she'd be delighted. The elderly woman held her hand and introduced her to one person after another as they made their way slowly toward the doorway.

"My dear." The lawyer came and put his arm around her in a fatherly way. "How nice to have you with us. How are you making out? Those mongrels let you in?"

"Bertha welcomed me from the beginning, but not Job. I might still be sitting in my car in the driveway if Tommy Gilbert hadn't rescued me."

The banker slipped past them, nodding to Emily.

"Mr. and Mrs. Chamberlain—Miss Emily." Hilda Gilbert introduced her to the minister and the organist at the doorway.

"I didn't have a chance to speak to you after the service Friday," Emily said. "I liked it. You have a beautiful voice, Mrs. Chamberlain."

The minister's wife smiled and expressed her thanks.

"I hear you're staying in the house," the minister said. "We visited Mr. Darrow a few times, but he didn't seem quite comfortable with a pastor my age."

"He made you co-executor of his will."

"I wish he hadn't. I don't know anything about legal matters. Thank goodness for Mr. Yost who has agreed to tell me whatever I need to know in order to do what Mr. Darrow expected me to do."

Mrs. Gilbert clung to the railing and leaned heavily on Emily as they descended the few steps to the walk in front of the church. Right in front of them stood the large middle-aged typist Emily had seen in the lawyer's office. She looked straight into Emily's face and then turned away, a deliberate snub.

"I'm ashamed of you, Geraldine," Hilda Gilbert scolded.

Her eyes lit up and she pulled Emily along the brick walk toward a tiny old lady with legs bent to form parentheses. "Josie, I want you to meet our new neighbor, Miss Emily. This is my oldest friend in the whole world, Josie Peck. She has dinner with us every Sunday. Ruth went along home and Miss Emily is going to drive us."

The old women chattered away in the loud voices of the slightly deaf all the way home. Mr. Gilbert ran out of the white clapboard farmhouse as they drove into the yard. The elder Mrs. Gilbert's fat was distributed all over her body. Her son's was concentrated in his stomach, which protruded over his belt. He greeted Emily in a booming voice, told her to call him Gil, and helped his mother and her friend up the walk.

At the door Ruth Gilbert kissed Josie and shook hands with Emily again. "Dinner will be ready in half an hour," she called as she scurried back to the kitchen.

Gil ushered Emily to a chair in the corner of the room, pulled up a hassock for himself, and announced that he wanted to talk with her about the ten acres.

"What ten acres?" Emily asked in a bewildered tone. Gil explained that years ago, while Peter was in Alaska, Gil had begun to plant corn on ten acres of cleared land on the Darrow property.

"I do truck farming and I raise sweet corn there," he explained. "Every summer while he was gone, I went in a couple of times with my tractor and mowed the weeds around his house. Wasn't much to pay for ten acres of land, but it was all I could think to do. The Rileys kept the place in repair. When he came back he told me to go on raising my corn there and I did. He still wouldn't accept rent, so I just kept on mowing and we supplied him with all the vegetables he could eat and Ruth made him pies. Boy, did he like Ruth's pies! Now you own the land and we'll have to make some other arrangements, that is, if you'll let me plant again this year. I've been checking around and farm land rents for—"

Emily interrupted him. "I don't know where the land is, but if Mr. Darrow let you farm it, I'll let you farm it."

"Are you planning to stay?"

"At least through the summer. Then I'll have to see. Mr. Riley is going to come next week to tell me what repairs should be made. The truth is, I don't have money for repairs. If the house needs a lot, I'll have to sell out. But you can definitely plant corn this summer."

"Thank you. I'll keep your lawn mowed and give you all the vegetables you want and Ruth will bake pies."

"No pies," said Emily firmly.

"Wait till you taste the one we're having today. Besides, you could stand a little meat on your bones.... You want to walk the lines after dinner?"

What was he talking about? "Is that anything like walking the plank?" she asked.

Gil slapped his thigh and laughed heartily before he explained he was suggesting that they walk the boundaries of her land, all clearly marked with surveyor's stakes.

As they went in to dinner, Emily saw Job and Bertha bound out of the woods, sniff around her car, and lie down beside it.

"Never thought Job would accept you," Gil said as soon as he had finished saying grace.

"He growls if I get too close, but Bertha sleeps right beside the bed."

"Peter always had dogs," Josie sighed. "Remember the pair of Irish setters? Used to come every afternoon to wait for him at the high school gate."

"Beautiful dogs and beautiful girls," Hilda said. "He kept his dogs but he changed girls with the seasons. My season was the winter of 1914. That was a brutal winter but we didn't mind. We skated on the pond and went for sleigh rides...."

"Mine was the spring of 1919," interrupted Josie. "I remember he brought me violets. Said they matched my eyes." The old lady giggled.

44

"What a pair of femmes fatales," Emily laughed.

"Not like you," said Josie wickedly. "I'm glad you weren't around then. You'd have been as bad as those girls who came every summer and snatched him away from us. How we hated those summer girls with their beautiful dresses and their weekly trips to the beauty parlor."

"Different girl every summer for Peter. I wonder why he never married one of them. I got married and you went off to college and came back to teach school, and still Peter was courting a different girl each summer. Remember the last one? She came to visit the parsonage during the winter—from the south. Such a pretty girl and she just dripped honey."

"And then?" encouraged Emily.

"Then she went off. Right after that Peter started building his house, and the next thing we knew he was gone. I'd always hoped he was building that house for you, Josie."

"So did I." Josie laughed. "And so did a half-dozen other girls in town. We all thought that when he finished his house, he'd ask one of us to be his wife. We were ninnies."

"He was gone for almost fifty years. Can you believe that? I wonder if he was married in Alaska. I asked him but he didn't answer me. He never did talk much. And now he's gone. Poor, dear Peter." Hilda wiped a tear from the corner of her eye with her napkin.

Emily did full justice to the pot roast, vegetables, and gravy and then to the apricot pie. She helped Ruth with the dishes and they talked about the Gilberts' children and grandchildren. "Tommy was an afterthought," she said. "A very happy afterthought."

Gil produced a box of boots and told Emily to try to find something that would fit, because the woods would be muddy. Ruth gave her an old raincoat that came almost to her ankles; it would protect her from

45

the underbrush. At last they were ready, Gil, Tommy, Ruth, and Emily, with Bertha frisking along beside them and Job at a distance.

They walked along what had once been a stone fence. "Everything on the far side of the fence belongs to you," Gil explained.

All of the land behind the Gilberts' house and small yard was plowed. They stopped to examine the peas and the asparagus that were pushing through the soil. Beyond was a huge strawberry patch. The woods on the other side of the stone fence came to an abrupt halt and there were plowed fields on their left as well as on the right.

"This is the beginning of your ten-acre field," Gil explained. "Look through there and you can see your tower."

Tommy led them along the side of the muddy field toward scrubbier woods and the stake marking the southeast corner of her property. They turned left and walked along the edge of the field until they came to a marsh. Somehow Tommy knew how to get through it without getting soaked, and they were again in woods, intersected by what Gil said were beaver canals. To their left was the pond. All the way from the stake the land had been sloping downward. Now it began to rise. Eventually they came to the stake that marked the northeast corner and turned left again. Still they continued to climb until they were in a clearing that Tommy said was the professor's campsite.

"Who owns the woods around Mr. Darrow's property?" Emily asked.

"Don't know," said Gil.

"Once upon a time," Ruth began, as if she were about to tell a fairy tale, "all this land—yours, ours, and land to the north and the west—was owned by Darrows. That was in the early 1800s."

Then, she explained, when rich, flat land opened in the Midwest, farming these rocky hills became unprofitable and most of the Darrows moved on west. The land reverted to forest. Gil's father bought the old farmhouse and acreage from one of Peter Darrow's uncles. Peter's father, the lumberman, hung on to his sixty acres though he lived in town and never did anything with it. Some of the land along the road to the north had been sold off in smaller parcels. All the land up the hill to the back had been abandoned and was eventually sold for taxes at auction.

Gil's father had expected to buy it, but a woman from New York City was visiting that summer. She attended the auction, caught auction fever, and ended up outbidding Gil's father.

"She really thought she had something until she found that the entire parcel was landlocked," Gil laughed.

"Landlocked?" asked Emily.

"No access to any road," explained Gil. "Pop refused to sell her an easement through his property, and Peter was in Alaska so she couldn't buy an easement from him. There she was with a deed for about a hundred acres of useless land. We never saw her again. Don't know who owns it now. We hear that most of the plots north of the beaver pond are now owned by a builder from Pittsfield."

They walked to the road and followed it back to the Gilbert farm.

"You really think Peter Darrow owned all of this land?" Emily asked. "Mr. Wilson said he'd sold the beaver pond and that the land he left to me stops at the lane."

"I don't believe that," said Ruth bluntly.

"I don't either," said Tommy. "Last fall Mr. Darrow asked me to walk his lines with him. It took a long time because we had to keep sitting down to rest. He showed me all four stakes. He said that most of the land really belongs to his friends, the beavers."

"Well, at least your field seems to be on land I will

own so you just go ahead and plant your corn."

As they walked toward the house, Gil told her that he had spotted several trees that could be cut for profit.

"God made trees for people to build with," Tommy announced.

"And for birds to nest in." Emily was emphatic.

"I hope that wherever Peter is, he heard that answer," Ruth mused.

The dogs were waiting beside her car when Emily got ready to leave. "Race you home," she called as she climbed into her car, and they ran off through the woods.

As she turned into her lane she heard a furious barking and a pained yelp that caused her to bear down on the gas pedal. She turned into the driveway with a spray of gravel and braked beside a small open English car.

A man with black hair and a red face was swinging a large flashlight at the dogs and swearing. Bertha was assisting Job by barking furiously from a position safely behind him. Although a small rivulet of blood was running down the white side of Job's face, he was guarding with an intensity that made his performance the day Emily arrived look like a game.

"Drop that flashlight!" Emily shouted as she leaped from her car and ran to Job's side. "Poor Job," she crooned as she grabbed the dog's collar, hoping he would not turn on her.

"Poor me," the man snapped belligerently. "That dog is vicious. I should report him to the authorities." The man was young and might have been attractive if his squinty eyes had not been so filled with fury and his long jaw had not been shaded by a deep shadow. He got back in his car and put the flashlight on the seat beside him.

"Did Job bite you? Did he hurt you like you hurt him? You're the one who should be reported, beating a little dog who was only defending his property."

The man looked up into her face, down her body, and up into her face again. Then he grinned. "A spit-fire. A cute little spitfire. I like a woman with spirit. My name is LaRoux, J. Simon LaRoux. My friends call me Jay." He started to climb out over the top of the door.

"Don't get out," Emily commanded.

"But honey, if you are Miss Emily Stanoszek, lately of Boston, we have business."

"I am Emily Stanoszek and I don't do business with men who beat dogs."

"That's just a surface scratch, cutie." One side of his mouth twisted up into a cocky smile. "I want to make you an offer you can't refuse. I'll buy your house, the land surrounding it—about thirty acres, I believe—and pay you twice what it's worth."

"Why do you want it?"

"Because I own all that land up there." He waved toward the woods above the house. "I need access to it."

"It's not for sale."

"Okay, honey. You try living in that creepy old house for a while. I'll be back and you'll run to me with open arms and accept any offer I make. In the meantime, you'd better get rid of those dogs." He gunned his motor and drove off, spraying her with gravel.

Emily was shaking all over, but as soon as J. Simon LaRoux turned onto the highway, she began to laugh. He'd called her a spitfire. She'd have to tell Allison and Dr. Moffat that!

Still holding Job's collar, she pulled him toward the house and into the kitchen where he climbed wearily into his chair, looking more mournful than ever. She stood a moment wondering what to do about the dog's injury. Alcohol would sting and make him even more distrustful of her. Finally she got a rag which she ran under warm water.

"Now, Job," she said calmly. "You have to let me

look at what that awful man did to you. I know you don't trust me, but you have to believe that Mr. Darrow wanted me to take care of you."

While she talked to the dog, she wiped away the blood and examined the small bump on the side of his head. It was not serious, she decided. She went to her bedroom and broke a spear off one of her plants.

"This is aloe," she explained to the patient. "It's supposed to be a healing agent." The dog continued to eye her suspiciously as she squeezed liquid from the spear onto the place where the skin had been broken. "Do you feel better?"

Job climbed down from the chair and headed for the door.

"Thank you," she said to Job as she opened the door for him. "I do appreciate your effort to protect me." She reached down to pat him, but he turned and walked away.

Emily was going back into the kitchen when Job began to bark again. She looked out the window and saw a navy Cadillac pull into her driveway and stop where the sports car had stood just moments earlier.

"It's Grand Central Station," she said to Bertha as she ran out to grab Job's collar so that a beaming Wilbert Wilson could get out of his car.

"Emily, my dear. I dropped by to see how you are getting along and to help you search for the deed. How are you?" he asked as they walked up on the porch and into the kitchen, leaving Job to bark after them from the other side of the door.

Wilbert Wilson looked around the filthy kitchen without comment and then suggested that they search for the safe in the foundation and around the fireplaces. He pointed out that in case of fire the house would burn in an instant, but the cement areas would be fairly fireproof. Peter Darrow would know that.

Emily followed the lawyer down to the basement where he shone a powerful flashlight beam on the foundation walls and the base of the fireplaces. Then they went upstairs and looked around the fireplaces in the parlor, the library, and the front bedroom. Nothing.

"Where now?" Wilson asked, mopping his brow with a pristine handkerchief.

Emily shook her head.

"So let's forget it for today. I'll try to think of other logical places and you keep looking. Actually, Peter Darrow was not a logical man so the deed could be anywhere. Did you know that he *gave* his lumberyard away?" His small eyes darted nervously about the room, then lighted on Emily. "Now tell me about you. Have you been very lonely?"

"No, I've had lots of company. Keith Cavanaugh was here yesterday. He was angry because he hadn't heard about Mr. Darrow's death."

"Keith Cav...oh yes, the Williams College professor. Did he think he could camp out there again this year? Impossible. The owners will not allow it."

"Who do you think owns the pond?" Emily asked.

"Builders from Pittsfield. I know they own it."

"When did they buy it?"

"Last winter." He looked around the grimy kitchen. "I certainly admire your courage and optimism, Emily. This house is going to be a real challenge."

"Do you know a man named J. Simon LaRoux?" She told him about her recent encounter with the man.

Yes, the lawyer knew LaRoux. He'd been buying up property all over town. "Take the word of your old Uncle Will and don't trust him for an instant. He's a shady character who is speculating on land around here hoping he can turn our little farming town into a mecca for tourists. If he comes to you again, tell him that I'm your lawyer and I'll handle your business affairs for you. I really do want to help you, my dear."

She held Job while the lawyer drove off. Then she changed into her jeans and started cleaning out a kitchen cabinet. She would make this place habitable!

By the next afternoon Emily was aching all over, but the kitchen was sparkling clean. She sat on the back steps contemplating her progress. The kitchen flooring was an attractive brick pattern and in good condition except right in front of the sink. But Peter's soiled chair was an eyesore. She wondered if Job would mind if she covered it with something she could wash. Then she'd hang pretty curtains and...

"Hello." Ruth Gilbert stepped out of the woods. "Just wanted to see how you were getting along. I also wanted to remind you to put your garbage out at the end of the drive the first thing tomorrow morning."

Emily led Ruth into the kitchen and was warmed by the older woman's approval. Ruth had never been beyond the kitchen so Emily took her on a quick tour of the first and second floors. With pride she pointed to the marble floor, the fireplaces, the window seat, and the barely visible stained-glass window.

"I had no idea it was so magnificent," Ruth breathed.

Back in the diningroom they stood in the bay and looked around. "I wish I had the money to furnish this room. It could be my living room. But I..."

Ruth began to talk about auctions—the first one would be Memorial Day weekend—and yard and garage sales. "But the place to begin is to talk to Buddy."

Buddy, Ruth explained, was the garbage man. He was mentally retarded, but he was able to drive the truck and he was conscientious. Buddy had an eye for useful items—and some that were hideous. If Emily made him understand that she needed furniture, he would bring her pieces from the dump. She could refuse anything she didn't want; there would be no problem there. Anything she did want would cost five dollars.

"He can't count or make change. Five dollar bills are known in Stonefield as 'Buddy bills.' On the first Tuesday of every month put a Buddy bill on the top of your garbage. His sister tells him which day he's supposed to collect. And if he brings you anything you like, pay him five dollars for it."

"And if he brings me something worth more than five dollars, can I give him two five dollar bills?"

"No, you'd only confuse him. We all feel protective of him. He is ugly and very, very slow, but he's gentle as a lamb. Don't worry if you see him down by the pond. He loves the beavers. Now, back to this room. You'll need curtains or drapes. Mom and I are planning a trip to a fabric mill later this week. Sometimes you can pick up bargains there. Want to come along?"

They made a date. When Ruth was gone, Emily made herself another dinner of bacon and eggs, soaked a long time in her tiny tub, and eased her aching body into the bed before it was totally dark outside.

Chapter Four

Emily was up with the birds the next morning, stiff but happy as she recalled the joy she had felt showing her house to Ruth Gilbert. She dragged the cans of garbage to the end of the driveway and then got out her electric coffee maker and filled it. Eddy Riley's father had called the day before to say he would be out to inspect the house, and she wanted to have plenty of fresh-perked coffee ready for him.

The dogs announced Mr. Riley's arrival. He was obviously a friend. He said a brief "good morning," looked around the kitchen with silent approval, and strode toward the back stairs. Emily tagged along behind him with a clipboard. He climbed directly to the attic, which turned out to be a huge open space with windows on all four sides. The beams and rafters were exposed and light slipped in through tiny slits in the side walls. Something swooped and fluttered over Emily's head. She ducked and cried out, then stifled the cry with the back of her hand.

"Just bats." Riley cast the beam of his flashlight along a rafter where dozens of little furry bodies hung upside down. "Lots of them."

Emily shivered and followed closely behind Riley as he stepped through the doorway to the tower room. It was lined with windows and rose to a roof that looked like an inverted funnel. Trying to forget the bats, she thought about her favorite fairy tale in a beautiful book that Grandpa had given her the first Christmas after she went to live with them. "Rapunzel, Rapunzel, let down your golden hair," the prince had called to the young woman trapped in the tower. Emily would have to let her hair grow so that the prince could climb up her braid and rescue her.

She stood transfixed by her own whimsical thoughts until Riley strode back to the stairway and down to the second floor. He went in each room, peering in every nook and cranny. He lay on his back to look at the pipes under the sinks and got down on his hands and knees to look into the fireplace in the master bedroom. He scribbled a few lines in a small notebook but said not a word. Emily followed along silently. He went through the downstairs rooms just as carefully. In the little bathroom he finally spoke.

"Eddy says you're going to paint this yourself. Ever painted anything?"

"No, but I bought a book at your store on home maintenance, and yesterday I bought the stuff they recommended for filling cracks."

He looked at her skeptically but said nothing. In the basement he stuck his knife in one of the beams and whistled. He went to a metal box and flipped a switch, examined the water heater and the huge furnace.

"We can't find the deed to the property," Emily said tentatively. "I've been told that if there's a safe it would probably be down here…"

"There is a safe. My dad said it took four men to lift it. He knew where it was. Said it was Peter's secret." He walked all around the foundation and cast his flashlight beam into every rough spot. "Not here. Let's try around the fireplaces upstairs."

He circled the outside of the house, then went back to the kitchen.

"I'll tell you what I found; I don't have time for written reports."

"Coffee?" She poured two mugs of coffee and brought them to the kitchen table.

"Best-built house I ever saw." Riley began his report. "Hemlock two-by-tens."

"That's good?"

"The best. But the cherry tree on the east has to go because it's damaging the foundation. I'll fell it and truck it to the mill. Give you half of whatever they pay me."

"What's it worth?"

He shrugged his shoulders. "Five hundred, maybe more."

"Dollars? For one tree?" she asked in disbelief.

"It's furniture quality."

"I don't know if I can sell it. We can't settle the estate until we find the deed. Some people think Mr. Darrow owned the beaver pond, and some people say that a group of builders in Pittsfield own it."

"Peter owned it." Mr. Riley continued his report, noting that the house would be impossible to heat in the winter. "We could insulate this part." He indicated the kitchen, the small bedroom, and her new sitting room as well as the rooms above them.

"What about the upstairs baths and lights?"

"The bathrooms never have been used. They're probably as good as when they went in. But don't turn on the water till you need it. Your water comes from a gravity spring up there." He indicated the woods behind the house. "I put in a new pipe from the spring to the house when Peter came back. You've got good water. We put in a new electric box and wiring for this part, but the rest of the wiring..." He shrugged his shoulders. "It's not up to code."

He took her to the basement and explained the electric box to her while she made notes. Then he led her to the diningroom and said that the damaged plaster was his responsibility and that he'd send someone to fix it and the rotten boards on the porch.

"Want the boards off the windows?" he asked.

"Yes, please."

"Okay, but leave the windows on the third floor covered."

Emily would like to have had all the boards removed, but Riley was telling, not asking.

"What about the bats?"

"Get rid of them and you'll have more mosquitoes."

"But they could be rabid," she said in a worried tone.

"Nah. We'll close them out if we repair the roof and fix up the third floor. For now they won't bother you."

Riley was wrong about that. Just knowing they were there bothered her, but she didn't say so.

She thanked him as they walked toward his truck. There was a rumble and an unmistakable fetid odor as an ancient truck came slowly into view belching smoke.

"Hi, Buddy," Riley called, as a man of indeterminate age with a huge head and a stocky body set on top of two stubby legs jumped out of the cab. He heaved Emily's garbage cans—the ones it had taken all her strength to drag—up in the air and emptied them on top of the pile.

"Ruth Gilbert said he might help me find furniture so I could turn the diningroom into a sitting room," Emily whispered to Riley.

"Sure thing." He motioned to Buddy with an exaggerated gesture. The trash man shuffled toward them, staring at Emily. "This is Miss Emily. She lives here now."

"Pleased to meetcha." Buddy raised his hand, pulled off his glove, and touched Emily's hair gently. "Pretty." He grinned, revealing all six teeth in his mouth.

"Very pretty," said Riley. "But don't touch."

Buddy drew his hand back as if he had been struck.

Riley propelled him toward the house and led him to the empty diningroom.

"She needs furniture. Chairs." Riley squatted to a sitting position. "Tables." He pretended to eat. "Lamps." He pretended to pull a light chain.

Buddy grinned and nodded. When they were outside he shuffled quickly to his truck, opened the door on the passenger side, and pulled out a small wicker table. Having once been white, it was now almost black with dirt and grime. He placed it carefully in front of Emily.

"It's sturdy," Riley said, putting his hand down on the top to test it for strength. "You could scrub and spray paint it."

"Oh yes. Wait right here." She ran into the house and got her wallet, dismayed to find that she had a ten and a few ones but no five. Riley changed the ten for two fives from his wallet and she gave Buddy one of the fives. "Thank you," she said gratefully. "Thank you very much."

"You like?"

"Oh yes. I love it. I really do."

Satisfied, Buddy shuffled off to his truck promising more.

"More than you can use," Riley laughed. "Don't buy anything you don't want." He drove off.

Having cleaned the bedroom, bathroom, and kitchen, Emily decided to tackle the butler's pantry. It was a long, narrow room with four doors that led to the kitchen, the diningroom, the basement stairs, and the back stairs. One entire wall was covered with cupboards and drawers. One cupboard was stuffed with graying sheets and pillow cases which seemed to be in good condition. Emily put them to soak in bleach and detergent in the bathtub.

The next drawer contained papers. Under canceled checks, mostly made out to the grocer, was a colored snapshot. She recognized the dog in the picture first. It was Ebony. Then she recognized herself, playing with the dog in front of the Moffats' house in Wellesley. Questions choked her.

She removed the drawer and took it to the kitchen table where she sat down to examine each piece of paper, putting the checks in one pile. She opened the first envelope and pulled out a tax bill. The second was from a detective agency in Boston. She stared at it and gasped as she realized that it was about her:

Dear Mr. Darrow:

As per your instructions, we have investigated the whereabouts of Grace Ann Gresham Potter and her heirs.

Mrs. Potter died in 1981 and is buried at Green Forest cemetery next to her husband, Thadeus Potter, who died in 1972. Mr. and Mrs. Potter had one child, Grace Ann Potter Stanoszek. Mrs. Stanoszek and her husband were killed in an accident in 1967. Their only child, Emily Stanoszek, was raised by the Potters, attending Miss Palmer's School for Girls and Wellesley College.

Although Mrs. Potter lived well all her life, she died deeply in debt. Miss Stanoszek now lives with a professor and his wife who pay her tuition and provide her with a home. In exchange, Miss Stanoszek cares for their children and does light housekeeping. She is described by the professor as being sweet tempered, extremely shy, loving to the children, and good with the animals. He is the only person to whom I spoke directly. I did not reveal your name. He said Miss Stanoszek is an above average student. She will receive a liberal arts degree in May.

Enclosed is a snapshot which I took from my car. As you will see, she is very pretty—small, slim with short reddish blond curls.

Our bill for services rendered is enclosed. Do you wish us to keep track of Miss Stanoszek's whereabouts when she leaves Wellesley? We will be happy to do so at our regular per diem rate....

In the same envelope was another letter.

Dear Mr. Darrow:
Miss Emily Stanoszek now shares an apartment in Boston with Miss Allison Moore, a classmate at Wellesley. She is employed as a receptionist in an accounting firm. See addresses below. Bill for services is enclosed....

Emily's first reaction was one of anger. A detective had been digging into her past, spying on her, taking pictures of her! It was a humiliating violation of her privacy.

She sat with her hands clenched and her lips pressed tightly together. Was it possible that the aloof old man who had given her the book of fairy tales was not her real grandfather? Or worse, was the vaguely remembered man with the scratchy mustache not her father? Who was Peter Darrow? Who was Emily Stanoszek?

She worked like a robot, mechanically sorting the papers into neat stacks. Suddenly there was a terrific flash and then a clap of thunder. Immediately the dogs began whining and scratching at the door. She let them in silently. The wind whistled around the corners of the old house as rain poured from the sky.

Emily continued her work until she had arranged all the canceled checks in order according to date. There was no deed among the papers, but what did it matter? She could not stay here. She didn't want to stay here. Peter Darrow, whoever he was, had actually hired a detective to spy on her.

Premature darkness fell and the rain continued to

beat against the windows. She switched on the radio and turned up the volume, hoping to drown her thoughts. She was alone, disconsolately alone.

All the life she could remember she had tried to please Grandma and Grandpa Potter because they were her family. Were they really her grandparents? Grace was surely her grandmother. Everyone always said they looked exactly alike. But who was Grace? She had been so proper. She wore clean white gloves every time she went out, reacted with perfect horror upon hearing a swear word. Had this Grace had an affair with Peter Darrow? *Impossible.*

She got out the papers she had brought with her from Boston. Grace and Thadeus Potter had married the same year that Peter Darrow had moved to Alaska—1929. Their only child, Grace Ann, had not been born until five years later. Could Peter have returned from Alaska and had an affair with Grandma Grace after her marriage? Could there have been a previous pregnancy?

She, Emily, was born ten months after her parents' marriage. Could the wedding license in front of her be a fake? Was that wonderful man who came to her in her dreams someone other than her father? What did she know of him, after all? What did she know of her mother?

The answer was—almost nothing. Her grandparents had not approved of Emily's mother's marriage and had cut their only daughter out of their lives. They referred to her father, on the few occasions they spoke of him, as "that immigrant." Emily had wrapped her few memories of him in satin and carried them close. She remembered riding on his shoulders as he galloped wildly around the living room. She was frightened but she did not want him to stop. She remembered him tickling her tummy with his mustache and squeezing her in his arms until she hurt. Were these pictures of other little girls and their fathers that she had adopted to comfort herself in her loneliness?

As for her mother, her memories were even less vivid but somehow comforting. Once in a department store she had caught a fragrance and suddenly remembered her mother braiding her long blond hair. Emily had gone to the perfume counter and sniffed bottle after bottle until she identified it, an inexpensive scent like flowers. Emily had bought a bottle that she never used; she just opened and sniffed it when she was lonely or troubled. All she had of her mother was in a bottle of scent.

Nothing made sense. Nothing at all. Bertha laid her head in Emily's lap, her liquid eyes filled with sympathy. Emily fed the dogs, ate a piece of bread without bothering to butter it, and went to bed—a bottle of cologne opened on the table beside her.

Emily awoke to a knocking on the door and dazzling sunshine streaming in the window. She pulled on her robe and opened the door to Buddy who stood on the porch, beaming, with a large round table on his back. She tried to smile and say "good morning," but the words stuck in her throat. How could she explain that she had decided to leave, that she didn't need his contributions? He looked so proud that she let him in. Staggering under the weight of the table, he eased it through the doorways and set it down under the chandelier in the diningroom. The top was badly scarred, so was the single center pedestal, and it was black with grime. It fit the room.

"You like?" Buddy asked eagerly. "You like?"

"Yes, Buddy. It's really lovely." She handed him five dollars and he left grinning.

She drank several mugs of coffee and prepared the last of the bacon and eggs. When she went to take a bath she saw that the sheets were still soaking. She rinsed them and took them outside where she draped them on the bushes to dry. They were sparkling white, a small miracle that pleased her.

Bathing quickly, Emily dressed and bundled up the papers she had found, determined to take them to Mr. Yost at the bank. She'd always depended on the kindness of strangers. Why change now? She'd tell him she was planning to move on and ask him what to do about the dogs. He would know if she could trust them with that irritating professor.

She stood just inside the doorway of the bank to get her bearings.

"…she does have lovely hair. I'm not saying she doesn't, but she's still a bastard." It was the lady from the lawyer's office. The woman to whom she was speaking giggled.

A man behind Emily cleared his throat and stepped around her. It was Calvin Chamberlain, the minister. He looked back at her with sympathy and then stepped toward the speaker.

In the meantime, an elderly voice crackled from the other side of the room. It was Josie Peck. "I will not have a former student of mine use language like that, Geraldine. If you have proof of what you say, then please be so kind as to use the more gentle, if old-fashioned term, love child. If you have no proof, you had best not speak on the subject." She looked up at the minister who patted her hand as if encouraging her to go on. "Remember that Peter Darrow was an honorable, a kind, a loving man. He gave this girl his most cherished possession. If he is in any way related to her, it is through love."

Mr. Chamberlain led Josie back to stand beside Emily. He hadn't said a word, but he had somehow endorsed every word the elderly woman had said.

The giggler stammered an apology, and Geraldine left the bank without a word. Josie suggested that Emily come to her apartment for a cup of tea.

Emily thanked Josie but declined. Then she turned

to Calvin Chamberlain and asked if he'd go with her to see the banker. "There's a question about a cherry tree," she said.

In the banker's office she handed over the papers she had found and explained that the cherry tree might be worth a lot of money but was damaging the foundation of the house. "It also bangs against the window—scary until I knew what it was."

Both of the executors agreed that she should go ahead and have it felled. Mr. Yost cashed her check from Allison's fiancé, so she stopped at the grocery store to buy something good to eat for a change.

When Emily arrived home, she found that during her absence a "No Trespassing" sign had been driven into the ground opposite her lane. She pulled it up, surprised at her own strength, and threw it into the bushes. Then she gathered and folded her lovely white sheets. She decided no mean-spirited gossip would keep her from enjoying her house. If she were Peter Darrow's love grandchild, so be it.

A little later, wearing an old shirt of Peter's, she scraped all the flaking paint in the bathroom. She filled the cracks according to the directions in her book. Then she poured primer into the tray and began to paint with the roller. The paint dropped in great blobs onto the drop cloth and her nose and her sneakers. Paint oozed down the handle of the roller, onto her hand, and down her arm. She tried the brush with the same dismaying results.

The dogs began barking and there was a knock at the door. She listened for a growl. Hearing none, she shouted "Come in" and went on with her work.

Laughter filled the passage and she turned to see Eddy hooting and slapping his thigh. "Dad was right," he was finally able to say. "You can't learn to paint from a book. If you could see yourself. Or maybe you meant to cover yourself rather than the walls."

Emily bristled. "I'll get the knack of it. See how well

I've filled the cracks. I learned to do that and I'll learn to paint. I may be a little sticky..." That was the understatement of the year, and Emily began to share Eddy's laughter.

He took the roller from her, wiped off the handle with a rag, and began to apply paint, rolling it out on the tray and then spreading it in long sweeps across the ceiling. It looked so simple the way he did it. When the ceiling was done, he showed her how to use the brush to fill in the corners.

"I've come to repair the verandah and to take down some of the window boards," he announced. "The plasterer will be here tomorrow."

Friday was the day selected for the visit to the fabric mill. Ruth Gilbert arrived with her mother-in-law and Josie Peck sitting together in the back seat. Emily invited them in to see her house. Hilda Gilbert handed Emily a rag rug just the right size to cover the worn spot in front of the kitchen sink. She'd made it herself. It was perfect and Emily said so. The plump old lady kissed her.

"I can't believe what you've accomplished," Ruth said when they had completed the tour of the back rooms.

In the diningroom they examined her two "Buddy" tables and agreed that light blue would be a pleasant color for the walls above the chair rail. Then Emily flung open the swinging door to the great hall. The women stepped through the doorway and gasped in unison. Splashes of color from the magnificent stylized garden scene in the stained-glass window mingled with clear light from the windows on either side of the huge door to reveal the carved stairway and black and white marble floor.

"I had no idea," Josie whispered.

Their reactions to the parlor and the library were equally satisfying, and Emily found herself bragging

66

that Edward Riley had said it was the best-built house he had ever seen. She apologized for the dust that clung to everything, although it did not diminish the splendor of the rooms.

The old ladies chattered enthusiastically about the house all the way to Pittsfield. At the Berkshire Atheneum, a modern library at the edge of the commons in the center of Pittsfield, Josie got out. She wanted to browse there until they returned from their shopping. She asked Emily if she needed any books and agreed to look for a beginner's gardening book. Then she offered Emily the use of her portable sewing machine.

The mill was a gold mine and Emily left with yards of plain white cotton, denim, and several remnants.

When Ruth drove her home, Emily found Eddy putting a second coat of paint on the verandah he had repaired. He ran to the car to help her with the bundles of fabric and the books Josie had selected for her.

"That's a nice young man," Hilda whispered.

Emily didn't reply, but when Eddy invited her to go to the movies on Saturday night, she accepted.

Gil brought both his son and a lawn mower early Saturday morning, and Tommy and Emily spent the day outside. With the garden guide Josie had selected propped up on the railing of the verandah, Emily pruned back the bushes around the house. She raked away the accumulation of dead leaves under them. Tommy stopped mowing long enough to point out a special bush.

"It's a peony," he said. "Mr. Darrow had me fertilize it last fall so it would be nice for you this spring. It'll bloom in June, he said."

By the end of the afternoon, Emily's house looked manicured. *You're getting house-proud, old girl,* she warned herself as she stood back admiring her work.

She had eaten her dinner and was dressing for her date with Eddy when the dogs barked. She threw on her bathrobe to open the door for Eddy; it was the professor.

"Always wear a bathrobe?" he asked, looking her over from head to toe.

"Always," she said firmly. "I just sit around all day watching TV and eating bonbons. Why should I get dressed?"

"So who fancied up the yard?" he asked, looking over her shoulder into the kitchen. "And who scrubbed this kitchen?"

"My staff—the gardeners, the maids. It is, of course, difficult to find competent help these days but I have been able to round up a quite adequate staff of six. I've given them all the night off."

He laughed heartily. "I really came to tell you that I'm setting up camp now and to ask you who posted the 'No Trespassing' signs "

"I have no idea but *I* pulled it out."

"It? There were six of them when I arrived and *I* pulled them all out. You really didn't put them up yourself?"

"I did not," she replied firmly.

"I believe you. Truce?" He held out his hand, grinning.

"Truce." Emily found herself staring into his deep blue eyes as they shook hands.

"So why don't we…" He stopped as a car pulled into the driveway; a door slammed and Eddy, wearing a sport coat and tie, ran up on the porch.

"Hi, Eddy. I'll be with you in a minute."

Eddy shook hands coldly with the professor.

Without another word, Keith Cavanaugh turned, calling to the dogs.

Emily ran to the bedroom and slipped into the flowered cotton skirt and pink T-shirt lying on the bed. She put her feet into high-heeled sandals and picked up a sweater. They went to a funny movie in Pittsfield and then had hot fudge sundaes. At the door, Eddy kissed her gently.

She'd had a lovely, comfortable evening with Eddy. Why then did she fall asleep wondering if Keith Cavanaugh would stop in again soon?

The next two weeks were satisfying to Emily. She cleaned and painted and sewed, beginning with Job's chair. Job eyed the new denim throw on his chair suspiciously, whined and then climbed onto it, sniffed, and settled down. His eyes were still sad. He never showed Emily any sign of affection, but he no longer growled or bared his teeth at her.

Buddy produced a wrought iron floor lamp which Eddy rewired for her. Buddy also offered her a brass figurine of a nude female figure with a strategic drape, which Emily refused. Then she worried that Buddy would stop bringing her treasures from the dump, but the very next day he brought her a rocking chair. When Calvin Chamberlain and his wife came to call, she was able to serve tea in her sparkling, if sparsely furnished, sitting room.

Eddy took her to dinner in Great Barrington one night, then he invited her to the movies again. She had friends and a home. The sounds of the house no longer frightened her. Job was a dedicated guard and Bertha was a loving companion.

It was just a mile from Emily's house to the grocery store, and she now walked into town almost every day to watch the sleepy town awaken for the tourist season. The open-air market area opposite the lumberyard received a new layer of gravel. An awning went up over the restaurant's patio. Shops opened. "Guest House" signs appeared.

One afternoon, as she stood peering into the window of a recently unboarded shop, the woman behind the counter looked up, stared, and then waddled to the door. Her short dumpling figure was covered, throat to ankles, by a flowered cotton tent. Ropes of wooden and silver beads hung from her thick neck. Silver earrings dangled around her shoulders and her short black hair was brushed away from her face.

She stood in the doorway a moment then spoke. "Hello, Grace." Her voice was throaty. "My name is Nika Frieberg. I'm very glad to meet you at last."

Emily shook her head. "I'm not Grace. I'm Emily Stanoszek. But hello, anyway."

"Of course you're Grace. I painted your picture for Peter Darrow. I just heard that he died." She reached up and tilted Emily's chin toward the light. "My mistake. You're not Grace but..."

"My grandmother's name was Grace." Emily hesitated. "I'm Peter's heir but I never heard of him until I was invited to his funeral. It's the great town mystery, as you may have heard." She tried to laugh.

"Come in." The woman held the door and then closed it behind Emily. "My main gallery is in St. Petersburg. The summer before last I opened this as my summer gallery. I'd only been open a few weeks when an old man presented me with several cracked snapshots and a poorly colored studio photograph. He said he wanted a painting of the woman walking down the staircase in his house. He said her name was Grace. Business was so poor I agreed to try. Had I but known! I went to the house and sketched the outlines of the staircase in that gloomy hall. Wish I could have seen the stained-glass window with the light shining through it, but everything was boarded up....But perhaps you know that."

"I do. It's not now. You'll have to come see the window."

"Do you know anything about the picture?"

"It's in the back of the closet," Emily laughed. "The first night I saw it hanging in his bedroom I thought it was myself in a previous life. I hid it away and haven't looked at it since."

70

"Would you let me borrow it? There's a tidy market for portraits, but the problem is that the buyer takes his portrait and I never have anything to exhibit as an example of my work. I could put it in the window and—"

"Not in the window! You might just as well know that some of the local people think I am Mr. Darrow's illegitimate grandchild. I couldn't bear to think of them ogling that picture, but you may borrow it if you promise to show it to potential clients only."

"I'll agree to that. If it's any comfort to you, Emily, I know that Peter Darrow loved Grace and that he continued to love her in old age. I wish you could have seen what I went through to get the color of her hair to satisfy him. Now that I see your hair, I know what he meant when he talked about a halo of light."

Nika locked her shop and drove Emily home. As they approached the house with its gleaming white trim and sparkling windows, the older woman gasped. They walked through the kitchen and sitting room to the hall.

"Stunning," Nika breathed as she gazed at the window over the carved staircase.

"Amazing, isn't it, what soap and water and light can accomplish?"

"And a lot of elbow grease. I imagined Grace as a fragile flower. *Curly locks, curly locks, wilt thou be mine? Thou shalt not wash dishes, nor yet feed the swine...*"

"*...but sit on a cushion and sew a fine seam, and feed upon strawberries, sugar and cream,*" finished Emily. "A perfect portrait of my grandmother!"

"But you're not like that, are you? You're made of sterner stuff."

"I never thought I was. Actually I've always depended on strangers, and what is this house but the gift of a kind stranger?"

"Which you have proved to be worthy of." Without

71

being asked, Nika climbed the stairs and returned with her eyes twinkling. "Have you thought of renting rooms for the summer? Serve a simple breakfast and you can charge fifty dollars a night."

"I couldn't be ready this summer. If I decide to keep the house, I might do it next summer."

"You'll keep the house."

Emily pulled the painting from the closet without looking at it. Nika put it in her car and drove off.

Chapter Five

Ruth Gilbert had explained that everything began on Memorial Day weekend, including the gardens. There could be frost the week before but not the week after.

On Friday of the holiday weekend, Emily found flats of flowers banking the outside of the grocer's store. She bought a pink geranium and planted it on Peter Darrow's grave. Saturday morning she planted marigolds in front of her house. Then she set off on foot to attend the first auction of the season at the big barn just outside of town.

She was huffing up a steep hill on the main road when a pickup truck pulled up beside her and the door opened. "Want a ride to the auction?" It was Keith Cavanaugh. She smiled and climbed in. "You sure are dolling up Peter's house."

"Yes, I am." She was defensive. "I think it looks very nice."

"Why did you have the cherry tree cut?"

"Because the roots were damaging the foundation."

"Oh, I thought you might have been frightened by the noise it made banging against the house." He eyed her slyly.

"As a matter of fact, I barely noticed the noise." She was not a competent liar. "The tree was furniture quality and I used the money from it to have the trim painted—to preserve it." She spoke through clenched teeth.

He chuckled as he parked the truck by the side of the road. "We seem to be remarkably adept at raising one another's dander, don't we? Maybe we should heed the good book: *love thy neighbor.*"

"That seems drastic. How about tolerate thy neighbor?" She found herself laughing into his twinkling blue eyes. *They're such a deep blue,* she thought, *almost purple. Too bad his disposition isn't as attractive as his face.*

The auctioneer had not yet taken the stand so they roamed among the articles for sale. Emily knew that her total assets had dwindled to one hundred fifty-two dollars, but Mr. Yost had said she could borrow against the estate. Now that the tourist season had begun, she might find a job.

There was a wing-backed chair with slightly soiled green upholstery. She examined it carefully. Perfect for her living room, but twenty dollars would be the absolute maximum she would bid on it. There were some straight-backed chairs. None of them matched but she could use them with her round table. There was a porch swing, just made for her verandah. And there was Buddy's brass nude woman.

"Buddy offered that to me," she whispered to Keith. "Do you think the auctioneer paid five dollars for it?"

"Sure. You wait, you wise shopper." His voice was taunting.

The auctioneer stood on a platform at the end of the huge open tent. He blew into the microphone and started with a box of bric-a-brac that went for two dollars. Then his helpers brought a camp cot to the stand and raised it over their heads.

"And here we have a bed. What's more important to man's comfort than a bed? Sturdy flat springs. We'll throw in this nice thick mattress. Everything in top condition…just a slight rip in the mattress. What am I bid for this magnificent sleep inducer?" There was silence. "Do I hear fifty cents?"

Emily raised her hand tentatively.

"Fifty cents here," Keith shouted.

"I have fifty cents. Do I hear a dollar? A dollar there. Do I hear two dollars?"

"A dollar fifty," shouted Keith.

"A dollar fifty. Do I hear two? Two dollars. Two dollars. Going for one-fifty. Going. Going. Gone, to the man in the beard. Sleep in peace."

Everyone laughed. A helper came and took Emily's money, and Keith said he'd put the cot in his truck.

"Will it be safe?" she asked anxiously.

"You saw how many people were dying to buy it." He sauntered toward the front, and she watched him as he carried the bed and mattress toward the truck. He came back and stood examining books on a table.

More bric-a-brac was auctioned and then one of the odd chairs. Emily bid to five dollars and stopped. The chair went for eight. She bought the next chair for one dollar. It was dirty and the finish was chipped, but a fresh coat of paint would do wonders. When the helper brought it to her she sat on it.

The tent was crowded, and she soon lost sight of Keith. Better items were coming up—a lovely oak dresser, an Oriental rug, a four-poster bed. Then the wing chair. Bidding began at ten dollars. Emily bid fifteen. Someone bid twenty. She ached for the chair and bid twenty-five. Someone bid thirty, then forty, then fifty. At fifty the bidding stopped. "Going. Going." A muffled voice in the back called "Fifty-five." It was all over. Some horrible person had stolen her chair. She consoled herself with another side chair for two fifty. As she was paying for it, she saw Keith pushing his way toward her with a paper bag.

"Is this seat taken?" he asked, sitting on her newest acquisition. He opened his bag and handed her a cup of coffee and a sandwich. Unfortunately for her, Keith had returned to her side in time to see the brass lady put on the block. The bidding started at five dollars and rose rapidly to sixty-five. Someone actually paid sixty-five dollars for something she had refused at five!

"You could have been rich," Keith twitted her. "What a judge of *objets d'art.*"

"I still think it's hideous," she scowled.

"So do I," he whispered.

Emily bought the porch swing for eleven dollars. Keith bought a picnic table and two benches. "Anything else?" he asked.

She shook her head. She was ready to leave even thought there were still hundreds of items to be sold and the crowd was larger than ever. They walked to the truck, carrying the picnic table between them. She dropped her end and stared. Her green chair was in his truck.

"How?...Where?..." she stammered. "Did you bid against me?"

"I'd never do that. As a matter of fact, the people who bought it couldn't fit it in their car so I offered them twenty-five dollars for it and they were glad to be rid of it."

"Is that true?" she asked suspiciously.

"Cross my heart."

She gave him the money, thanking him profusely, unable to believe her good fortune.

"If you're really so grateful, you'll prove it." His voice was teasing. "Go to dinner with me tonight."

"How can I refuse?" She smiled warmly as he held the door of the pickup for her.

When they approached her house, Emily saw that a huge basket of purple petunias was hanging on one side of the front entrance to her verandah and a basket of yellow ones on the other.

"Look at those," she breathed. "Who could have put them there? They're perfect." She jumped out and ran to examine them more closely.

76

Keith unloaded the truck. "Where do you want this stuff?"

"On the verandah," she said. "Except for the chair."

She let herself in by the back door, ran through the house, and threw open the front door. Keith looked in and stared at the woman, whose vivid coloring was made even more striking by sunshine streaming through the stained-glass panes behind her.

"How do you like this?" she asked happily as she led him into her parlor.

"Nice," he said almost curtly, as he looked around. "Who did it for you? That poor besotted lad from the lumberyard?"

"I painted this room myself."

"No." He shook his head. "Not you. You're the kind of pretty woman who leads a man on until he kills himself for you. Then you dump him as soon as something better comes along. Peter and I both have had experiences with your kind. Poor Peter."

"You don't know what you're talking about, Dr. Cavanaugh. It's quite possible that that poor besotted lad, as you call him, hung those baskets for me, but I assure you I have worked like a dog—a horse—on this house, inside and out. And I'm proud of it. Proud! As for 'Poor Peter,' I never met him so I couldn't have led him on. It's possible that he may have been in love with my grandmother. I don't know. One thing I do know is that you are rude and judgmental and..."

"And I think we'd better cancel that dinner...," he said coldly.

"I agree!"

He turned and marched to the front door. Bertha ran to him eagerly. "In case you haven't noticed," he called back over his shoulder, "Bertha is going to whelp—in about a month, I'd guess. Her first litter. Don't suppose you'll want to play midwife so I'll just move her up to my camp."

"You leave that dog alone," Emily replied hotly. "I'll take care of her myself."

The door slammed.

Coming out of church the next morning, Emily stared down a main street crowded with tourists. Some had arrived in big yellow buses. Every parking place was taken.

The gravel area opposite the lumberyard had been transformed into a flea market. She walked happily among the stalls and bought a flat of impatiens. Chairs, similar to the two she had bought at the auction, bore price tags of ten dollars each. She bought a remnant of red, green, and blue striped fabric, hoping she could use it to turn her camp cot into a sitting room sofa.

Emily stepped into Nika's gallery; it was a mad house! Nika was struggling to answer questions, make change, and wrap packages all at once. She was having a run on small, framed floral prints.

"Will someone answer my question?" a strident voice demanded. "Why are these pictures so expensive? They're all alike, just different colors."

Nika looked at the woman and shrugged her plump shoulders. She could not get away from the counter where tourists were demanding her attention. She ran her hand through her short black hair in a gesture of helplessness.

Still holding her plants, a paper sack, and her purse, Emily made her way to the impatient customer. Quietly she explained that they were silk screens and that the artist changed the colors as he printed. She also pointed to the strokes of color that had been brushed onto the finished prints.

"While the basic design is the same on several of these, you will notice that no two are exactly alike. Furthermore, they are signed by the artist. They're rather reminiscent of Kandinsky, don't you think?"

Nika grinned at her and nodded. "You're hired," she mouthed silently.

Emily ran to the office, dropped her purse and purchases, and ran back to the demanding tourist, her first customer. After that Emily took up a position behind the counter, wrapping packages and taking money while Nika worked with the serious buyers. Before long her feet hurt and Emily began to wonder about closing time. Finally she kicked off her shoes and padded around barefoot—until a huge man stepped on her toe.

By seven o'clock the gallery was beginning to clear. At last Nika pulled the shade on the glass door and put up the "Closed" sign. She grabbed Emily in a giant bear hug and kissed her on the cheek.

"Reminiscent of Kandinsky!" she shouted. "What a line! Here, help me count the cash and get the bank deposit ready and then I'm taking you across the street for the best dinner on the menu."

As soon as they were seated, Nika came right to the point. "Do you want a part-time job?"

Emily nodded.

"So tell me something about yourself."

"I graduated from Wellesley last spring. Majored in art history, which I loved. I found out later that I should have majored in computers if I wanted to find work."

"Ever had a job?"

"I was a receptionist for an accounting firm in Boston but…" Emily hesitated and then went on bravely. "I was terrible and I was fired. I'm too shy for a job with the public."

"You? Shy? You stepped right up to that customer and told her about silk screens. I need help on the weekends and for a few hours during the week if I get commissions for portraits. I'll pay minimum wage plus commission."

Emily sat smiling to herself. She *had* walked right up

to that woman and started talking. And yesterday she'd told Keith Cavanaugh a thing or two. Without realizing it, she was becoming more assertive.

They were discussing items in the shop and finishing their dinners when J. Simon LaRoux approached their table. "Good evening, ladies. May I join you for coffee?"

"Hi, Jay. Want you to meet my new business associate, Emily Stanoszek. My landlord, Jay LaRoux." Nika smiled at both of them.

"I've already met this adorable creature," he said, pulling up a chair and seating himself. Then taking Emily's hand, he held it as if he sensed her desire to run from him. "Your dog survived, I trust."

"He did," Emily said shortly, pulling her hand loose from his grasp.

Nika looked from one of them to the other, bewildered.

"I went to this sweetie pie's house on a mission of mercy..."

"Some mission of mercy," inserted Emily.

"I wanted to save her from the cares of that monstrous house she inherited. Before I could even see her, two vicious dogs attacked me. I had no choice but to give one of them a gentle tap. But that's all in the past, forgotten." He turned to Emily. "Shall we open negotiations? I'm prepared to offer you a price that will warm your cold, cold heart."

"I'm not interested," Emily said.

"You should see what's been accomplished out there, Jay," Nika said enthusiastically. "Emily has already brought the house to life. What do you think of this first weekend? Enough tourists to satisfy you?"

"Quite satisfactory. Your shop was crammed, the new leather shop next door did well, and my blue-haired lady was selling fake Victoriana as if it were the real thing."

"How are you coming with your plans for the restaurant in the old train station?"

"Railroad wants an arm and a leg so we're still negotiating, but I'll get it. I always get what I want." The waiter came to their table with two steaming bowls of bouillabaise, and Jay LaRoux got up and ambled out. Emily was glad to see him go.

After dinner, Nika drove Emily home where two hungry dogs ran to the car to tell her they felt neglected. "Are you sure those dogs are trustworthy?" Nika asked.

"Positive."

During the first weeks in June, Emily tried to push all thoughts of the odious Keith Cavanaugh out of her mind by concentrating on Eddy. He was a darling. He had actually blushed when she thanked him for the hanging baskets. When she had kissed him impulsively on the cheek, he had taken her in his arms and kissed her firmly on the mouth.

He put up the swing for her and hung a pillow behind the camp cot so that it looked somewhat like a couch. With the wing-back chair and the two new side chairs, her sitting room was sparsely but comfortably furnished. She was well satisfied with it and with her life. Furthermore, she was making enough money at the gallery for her day-to-day expenses.

Job came in to eat and to sleep in his chair. Otherwise he was out all day, rain or shine. Bertha, however, as her sides swelled, spent most of her time sleeping on the porch or lying close to Emily.

"I wish you'd tell me who the father is," Emily said. "Is it Job?"

Bertha did not answer.

One rainy afternoon Emily took Josie to the Berkshire Atheneum and applied for a library card. She checked out a number of novels—and three books about dogs. Then she stopped at the vet's and bought vitamins for Bertha and added them to the meaty stews she made to feed the mother-to-be. The books assured her that when the time came, instinct would take over and Bertha would give birth without assistance. A worried Emily hoped the books were right.

Mr. Yost phoned one morning to ask if she had found the deed. The estate could be settled if they could determine positively how much land was involved. Unfortunately, the registration had been lost in a fire in the county office in the 1940s. The tax collector said that according to her records, Peter Darrow owned sixty acres, more or less, and had paid taxes on those sixty acres last year and every year.

The same afternoon Wilbert Wilson phoned and asked if he could come out. Again she and the lawyer searched the house. She had been through every cupboard in the kitchen and the butler's pantry. He went through them again. They knocked on the walls in the living room in the best detective-story style. The lawyer searched for loose bricks and loose floorboards. There were no hollow sounds behind the paneling. The staircase seemed solid. They checked the closets upstairs and the bedrooms. Wilson even went to the attic to search.

"I give up," the lawyer said at last.

Emily offered him coffee and led him into her sitting room.

"You've worked wonders here," he said, looking around appreciatively. "This is a cozy room indeed, and the outside of the house is much improved. I imagine it's very lonely here at night—all those empty rooms and those bats. There are hundreds of them in the attic. Bats are usually rabid, you know. You want to get out?"

"No. I have a job at the gallery. I'm busy and happy here. It is lonely at night but I have Job and Bertha for company."

"Good. Still this is no place for a beautiful young woman. You never know who might be lurking about.

Besides you'd die of boredom here in the winter. You could never heat this house. I've talked with the Pittsfield Corporation. They're prepared to give you twenty-five thousand dollars for the property without the deed."

"It's not for sale," Emily said firmly.

"You drive a hard bargain. Remember, they already own the land on the other side of the lane. How about thirty-five thousand?"

"No."

"I might be able to get fifty thousand for you. You'd have to accept that. And you could stay here through the summer season. I'll call them and see what I can do."

"Don't. If I decide to sell, I'll let you know."

He patted her cheek. "Just as you say." She let him out through the big front door. "The squatter down there doesn't worry you? And Buddy wandering around there evenings?"

"Peter Darrow told Dr. Cavanaugh that he could camp there to complete his study. Buddy is harmless."

"No one knows anything about the professor. He seems to be a recluse. And there's a strange look in his eyes. I wouldn't trust him, Emily. As for Buddy—just don't let him get too close to you. You know, my dear, I feel responsible for you. I'd hate to have anything unpleasant happen."

Emily returned to the sitting room bewildered. She remembered how Mr. Riley had told Buddy not to touch her. She had thought of him as a little boy, but he was a little boy with a man's strength. Did he also have a man's sexual desires? That thought frightened her.

As for Keith Cavanaugh, was there something strange in his eyes? He said he was Peter Darrow's friend. Should she believe him?

She locked the doors carefully that night, as she did every night. She switched on the lights in her sitting room and sat down to watch television. She watched one sit-com and then another.

Crash! At the sound of shattering glass Emily felt the blood drain from her face. Bertha and Job began barking furiously. Her heart leaped into her mouth; she could neither swallow nor breathe.

Job ran to the swinging door between her sitting room and the hall, growling fiercely. Emily sat glued to her rocking chair. The dog pushed his flat nose against the door and finally managed to open it. He darted into the hall, and she could hear him throwing his body against the door to the parlor. At last she forced herself to her feet and ran on wobbly legs to the kitchen. She rummaged around frantically and found a flashlight.

Cautiously she opened the sitting room door and crept out into the hall. Bertha whined behind her. She threw open the parlor door and let Job lead the way into the dark room. He ran straight to a window where her flashlight beam picked up the outline of jagged glass around a hole in one of the small panes. A rock about the size of a golf ball lay in the center of the room. Job continued to bark and growl, Bertha to whine. Emily began to sob.

"Come on Job. Go out there and find whoever did this to us." She opened the front door and the dog bolted across the verandah, down the driveway, and into the woods toward the road. She stood listening to his frantic barking.

When it stopped, she bolted the door again, switched off the television and the lights in her sitting room and, as she had the first night, barricaded the pantry door with one of the kitchen chairs. She made herself a cup of tea and tried to soothe Bertha.

At last there was a scratch at the back door and she admitted Job, his coat shiny with sweat and his tongue hanging out. His sides heaved and his panting sounded like a locomotive. She wet a wash cloth and wiped him down with cool water, then she dried him with a towel. Job reached up and licked her face, the first sign of affection from the morose dog.

"Oh, Job," she cried. "You tried so hard. Who was it and why did they break our window? Did they mean to scare us? I've tried hard, too, you know. I've never lived alone before. I know I'm not alone. I have you and you are the best dog in the whole world. But how can we stay here when I'm afraid?"

Job licked her face again, and Bertha raised her heavy body and came and nuzzled her nose into Emily's hand. "I couldn't go away unless I took you with me, and Bertha can't travel just now. Tomorrow I'll ask Eddy to fix the window and put locks on the doors and windows so we can at least feel safe in the bedroom and kitchen. Get up in your chair and sleep now, Job." Bertha followed her to her bedroom.

"Thou shalt not be afraid of the terror by night or the..." Or the what?

Emily said the words over and over to herself as she tried to relax in her bed. Finally she switched on the bedside lamp and opened the drawer of the night table. She took out Peter Darrow's Bible and turned to Psalm 91.

Thou shalt not be afraid for the terror by night; nor the arrow that flieth by day.... There shall no evil befall thee, neither shall any plague come nigh thy dwelling. For he shall give his angels charge over thee, to keep thee in all thy ways.

As she put the Bible back in the drawer, the corner of a piece of paper slipped between the pages. She pulled it out and read these words, written in a shaky hand:

E: It gives me peace to imagine you caring for

85

my dogs and my house. I meant for us to be so happy here. P.D.

Who did he mean to be so happy? Were those the ramblings of a lonely, senile old man? Whatever he meant, he must have meant to be kind. She put the paper back in the Bible and switched off the light.

For he shall give his angels charge over thee. Maybe Job was her angel.

Late the next afternoon Eddy installed a piece of glass with a competence that amazed Emily. Then he put a heavy bolt on the door between the pantry and the sitting room and locks on all the windows in the kitchen, bedroom, and bath. When he had finished Emily brought him a tall glass of iced tea and they sat together on the swing.

"You really don't know who did it?" Eddy asked.

"I can't imagine."

"It could have been kids out for a lark. Parked their car on the road and came through the woods and…maybe they were drunk or high."

"If they were drunk, how did they manage to hit the window in the dark?"

"Maybe they were aiming for a tree and missed. Maybe it was just an accident."

"I hope so. Let's not talk about it any more."

He put his arm around Emily and she nestled against him. The edgy feeling that had lived with her all day ebbed away. He was small and wiry and three years younger than she, but he was very, very kind.

"Want me to spend the night?" he whispered in her hair.

She pulled back, alarmed. "No. Certainly not. I hardly know you."

He stared at her, looking confused and embarrassed. "I didn't mean that," he stammered. "I just… thought…if you are frightened, I could sleep here on

86

your couch thing…or in my truck…just so you wouldn't be scared. I wouldn't…"

Of course he wouldn't. "I'll be all right. Job protects me. Thank you, Eddy. You are one of the sweetest people I have ever met. I couldn't have managed here without you."

His mouth turned up in a bashful grin; he kissed her gently and left.

She was awakened the next morning by a knock at the door. The dogs had not barked. She threw on her robe and went to admit Buddy, who was standing on her porch with a dressing table like her grandmother had once had—two sets of small drawers separated by a shelf. The finish was badly marred and some of the drawer pulls were missing. While she was trying to decide if she wanted it or not, he shuffled back to his truck and returned with a large mirror which seemed to be in good condition. On a third trip he brought a large chest of drawers. She could antique them, she decided. She helped Buddy carry them up to the spacious front bedroom.

Later in the morning she went to the hardware store and bought a kit for antiquing and new drawer pulls. She was paying for her purchases when two young girls, just emerging from the acne stage, sauntered in looking like nervous colts. One of them was short and pudgy; the other was leggy, with thick chestnut hair that hung down her back. They giggled and the short one elbowed the leggy one in the ribs.

"Go on," she whispered.

Pulling in her already flat tummy and pressing her palms along her tight jeans she walked up to Eddy, ignoring Emily. "Hi Eddy," she said languidly, and then rushed on, "…party my house tonight…new records …can ya come?"

"I'm sorry, Judy," Eddy said kindly. "I've already made plans for tonight."

The girl scowled at Emily and bounced out of the store with her friend. At the door the pudgy one turned. "Bastard," she hissed at Emily and then ran.

Eddy ran after her.

"Pay her no mind," Mr. Riley whispered. "Just a kid. Jealous."

Emily gathered her packages and went home.

That night Eddy took her out to dinner. Neither of them mentioned the girls.

The peony burst into a mass of extravagant red and the marigolds spread into a border of bronze and gold. The weeds grew like—weeds. Emily tried to spend an hour every day in her yard. Freckles blossomed on her face, and she itched most of the time from sunburn. Her hair, she noticed, had grown lighter. She had little time to think about how she looked.

She did have her hair cut once at the local beauty parlor. As she entered the shop, all chatter stopped awkwardly. Knowing that she was the subject of town gossip made Emily uncomfortable. Still she had her house, her work, and Bertha and Job.

She worked every weekend and several weekdays at the gallery. She had occasional glasses of iced tea with Josie Peck.

The minister and his wife came to visit her when they heard about the rock that was thrown through her window. So did Jay LaRoux. He pulled up in his car one day as she worked outside.

"I hear that someone threw a rock through your window. Scare you? Ready to sell?"

"No," she said firmly, angered more by the lilt in his voice than his offer.

"So what does it take to convince you to get out?" The lilt turned to a shout as he gunned his motor and roared out of her lane.

She saw little of the Gilberts. They were busy from sunup to sundown in their gardens, and she only saw them when one of them dropped by with gifts of asparagus, peas, and lettuce.

Keith Cavanaugh occasionally drove down the lane when she was outside but he did not wave, let alone stop to talk. Evenings when she was lonely she sometimes stood in the bay window in her sitting room and looked across the beaver pond toward the light that shone in his campsite.

In spite of her loneliness, she began to turn down Eddy's invitations, feeling guilty because she could not return the growing affection that he seemed to feel for her.

Often she thought about leaving Stonefield as soon as Bertha could travel, but she knew that Bertha was not the problem, Job was. He was not young and this was his home. He needed space to roam, and he was still mourning the loss of his master. Besides, she had to stay until the estate was settled. Then she'd have to find a buyer, someone other than Jay LaRoux.

Chapter Six

July fourth was on a Monday that year. By Friday Stonefield was in high gear. It was stifling in New York and Boston so everyone who could possibly get away was heading for the beaches or the hills.

Osawa was conducting at Tanglewood; Pavoratti and Galway were performing. A famous movie actress was appearing in person at one of the theaters. A popular folk singer was drawing young people from hundreds of miles.

"No Vacancy" signs were sprouting on hotels, motels, guest houses, and campgrounds. The restaurants would be serving all day and far into the night. The Stonefield auction barn had announced a sale on Saturday that would feature Shaker chairs, Oriental rugs, and antique clocks.

The Stonefield flea market would be open all four days. It was the height of the strawberry season, and the Gilberts had hired young people to pick their crop. Ruth and Hilda Gilbert had made dozens of cakes so they could sell strawberry shortcake in addition to quarts of strawberries, snow peas, lettuce, radishes, and the first zucchini.

Nika and Emily had boxes of small framed prints ready to refill the shelves. They had covered every inch of wall space with large prints and original watercolors. In the window they displayed two first-class primitives—oil on boards—which Nika had picked up in a junk shop for twenty dollars each and hoped to sell for twelve hundred dollars. They set the best pottery in front of the primitives.

Emily had had a preview of summer in the Berkshires Hills on Memorial Day weekend. Still she was amazed at the hustle-bustle of the little town as it came alive to cater to the tourists and replenish its coffers.

As she dried her hair in the sun on Friday morning, Emily contemplated the weekend with both anticipation and dread. She had already discovered that she enjoyed selling art. Nika's collection was varied and in good taste. So she looked forward to the weekend, to showing and explaining, to selling and earning commissions.

Bertha was the cause of her dread. It was obvious the time for whelping must be near. Emily had brought a huge box from the grocer and set it up in the butler's pantry and lined it with layers of newspaper. Lying ready in the pantry were scissors, dental floss, a rough towel, a pail, and a book open to the chapter entitled "When Your Bitch Goes into Labor." Emily had all but memorized the book. The vet's phone number was stuck up on the wall beside her phone.

In spite of her preparations, Emily could muster no confidence in her ability as a midwife. She had never seen a birth. She was squeamish. The sight of blood made her feel faint; unpleasant odors made her nauseous. Bertha seemed equally uneasy. In spite of the heat, the big dog huddled close to Emily, following her from sink to refrigerator to stove, lying on her feet while she read, sleeping with her back against Emily's bed at night.

"You'll be all right," Emily tried to reassure her. "The book says—and you must believe the written word—that instinct will take over and you will know just what to do. If you're a good friend, you'll have the

92

pups quietly in the night and surprise me the next morning. Wouldn't that be nice of you? Think about it. That's just the kind of surprise I'd like best. If you'll have your pups without my help, I'll give you a treat. What would you like? A magnificent bone maybe? I'll even see that Job stays away so that you can enjoy it all by yourself. Is it a deal?"

The mother-to-be licked Emily's face, but she made no promises.

When she left for work at noon on Friday, Emily locked Job outside the house and Bertha inside, carefully closing her bedroom door.

"The book says you might like to give birth on my bed," Emily explained. "You must not do that. You'll be more comfortable in the firm box and the puppies will be safer. By the way, Bertha," she called as she locked the back door, "have you thought what you're going to do with the puppies? If you think I'm going to keep them, you're mistaken."

The dog whined.

Friday afternoon was fairly slow at the gallery, and Emily drove home at five to eat a sandwich while Bertha hauled her heavy body outside. Then Emily gave her another serving of her protein-rich stew and left with Job lying outside the door and Bertha inside.

Friday evening the weekenders were arriving, filling the shop. They were mostly lookers, not buyers, but Emily was kept busy.

Saturday Emily woke in a pool of perspiration. The day was going to be a scorcher. She watered the plants and baskets and sat down on the grass under a tree with a book. Bertha came and lay with her hot, heavy head in Emily's lap. Before she left for work, she tried to arrange the windows to take advantage of whatever breeze there might be. As she drove out to her lane, she saw several cars parked there, completely blocking the main road; so she drove back, locked her car, and whistled for Job.

"Everybody is trying to get to that auction, Job," she explained. "I'm depending on you to protect the property. Let the people park in the lane but do not let them in the driveway and especially do not let them up on the lawn. This is private property. You tell them that."

She hugged the dog and was rewarded with a wet lick. Then she hurried off through the woods toward town. When she turned and saw Job following her, she ordered him back to his post.

Languid customers strolled in and out all day long. Many were cross; so was Emily. Only Nika seemed to maintain her buoyancy in the stifling heat.

When Emily went home in the late afternoon to check on Bertha, Job was standing guard in the driveway. A man was opening the windows of a car parked in the lane.

"Some dog you've got there," he called to Emily. "I wanted to park off your driveway in the shade of that hickory tree but he wouldn't let me. He said it was private property. Well, I guess I should thank you anyway, old fellow, for letting me park in the lane, but it's like an oven in here." He got in his car and drove off.

"Good dog, Job," Emily crooned. "You can come in and eat. I think the auction is over."

Monday the sky was overcast and the air was absolutely still. According to the radio, this was the third day of a record-breaking heat wave. Emily drove back to the gallery after checking Bertha in the late afternoon and had no trouble finding a place to park. The local people were beginning to reclaim their town. Nika had had the best weekend ever.

Lightning flashed across the sky followed by a distant rumbling of thunder. The few customers who came into the gallery were serious shoppers. A young couple spent almost two hours selecting four framed silk screen prints for their law office. Emily made the sale while Nika totaled her books and prepared the night deposit.

When Emily left a little after nine, the thunder and lightning were closer and wind whipped the trees. A storm was brewing in her kitchen, too. Bertha was pacing the floor, back and forth, back and forth. She had not eaten the food Emily had put out earlier. Job ate it when he came in with Emily.

"Remember, Bertha, instinct will provide," Emily tried to reassure the big dog and herself. "I'll just go to bed and let you get on with it. You don't think that's fair? I suspect that Job is the father. Let him comfort you. Are you the father, Job?"

Job claimed no responsibility.

Emily took a shower and dressed in a pair of old blue shorts and a blue T-shirt. Bertha was shredding papers in her box. Job was watching with interest.

"You'd better go out before the rain starts," Emily told him. "Then sleep on Peter's coat on the back porch. If it rains hard, I'll let you in. In the meantime, I expect that Bertha would like to be alone."

Job left reluctantly, looking back at his miserable companion.

"This may go on for as long as twenty-four hours," Emily explained to Bertha as she stroked her head. "I'm going to bed but I'll be here if you need me."

Emily was awakened by a clap of thunder that seemed to be right over the house. Rain was beating on the window. Job was scratching at the door. She let him in and they checked on Bertha who was hauling her body around the box in circles. Job climbed into his chair and Emily went back to bed.

The next time Emily was awakened it was by whimpering and a dog's paw on her arm. She switched on the light. Job ran to the bedroom door and looked back, commanding her to get out of bed and follow him. He went to the pantry where Bertha was standing in the box, straining. She let out a cry. Job whimpered.

"Bear down," Emily encouraged as she ran to the suffering dog.

"Once more. I'm ready," Emily urged.

The dog cried and strained. When a tiny white puppy emerged from the sac, Emily examined it carefully.

"Oh, Job," she giggled with delight. "He looks just like you. He's even going to have one brown ear."

She laid the pup in the box and put her tools away. When she looked back in the box, Job was licking his son. Emily sat on the floor with her back against the wall and watched, tingling with anticipation. Job came and sat beside her while the pup nursed and Bertha rested.

The next two pups came quickly and without help from either the midwife or the father. Emily poured herself a glass of iced tea, and watched the rain running in rivers from the roof of her back porch. Bertha climbed wearily out of the box, drank a little water, and then went back to her pups.

"Is it all over?" Emily asked.

As if to answer, Bertha began straining again. She strained for a long time and made low, mournful sounds, but nothing happened. Job began to whimper. Emily checked the time. It was two-thirty. At three still nothing had happened. Bertha looked exhausted. At three-thirty Emily phoned the number beside the phone.

"This is a recording. The veterinarian is away for the weekend. In case of emergency, take your pet to the animal hospital in Great Barrington."

"Good gosh!" Emily cried aloud. "I can't get Bertha into the car. She can't walk and I can't carry her."

Emily thumbed through her book. "If the bitch labors for more than two hours, call your vet." Terrific advice. She'd already called the vet and he wasn't there. Bertha continued to strain and cry, but both the movement and the sound were weak. She rolled over on a pup.

Emily eased the pup out from under its mother and put all three pups in another smaller box. Bertha was too tired to care for them. Job went and licked each one as if to say "Daddy's here." The puppies slept, curled together.

Emily watched helplessly. "Dear God," she prayed, "Help Bertha. She's such a good dog and Peter Darrow loved her so. Don't let her die. Show me what to do for her." She turned her head so she could not see the dog's agony, but she could not block out her weak cries.

"We're doing the best we can," she whispered to the big dog who was panting heavily. Emily stroked the sweaty head, then she sponged her. Bertha tried to lick Emily's hand, but her tongue was too weak.

"Earlier tonight I thought there was nothing like motherhood," Emily said. "Now I think it's beastly." She looked at Bertha's sad, glazed eyes. "That's not the right attitude, is it? You have three lovely pups. One looks just like his father. Please, Bertha, just hang in there."

Bertha rose on trembling legs. Emily brought the water dish and held it while the dog lapped weakly. Then she began to strain again.

"Keith!" Emily exclaimed. Job came and looked up into her face. "He's a zoologist. He'll know what to do."

Emily threw on her raincoat, slicker hat, and boots, and ran out into the downpour. Her flashlight barely cut through the driving rain and the mud made running difficult. The lightning frightened her, but, she thought gratefully, the flashes did light up the area enough to keep her from becoming lost in the heavy underbrush.

Finally she reached the clearing near the beaver

pond. The big square tent loomed dark in front of her. Emily stood beside the zippered cloth door, shining her flashlight at it, and shouting to be heard over the rain.

To her heartfelt relief the door was unzipped and Keith's startled blue eyes peered out at her.

"Bertha's in trouble! She's having her puppies and she needs help. Please help me!"

"Wait a minute." The flap fell closed again. She huddled in her raincoat, impatiently, but it was only a couple of minutes before he stepped out, a raincoat flapping open above his boots and a powerful flashlight in his hand.

Without a word he set off for the house. It was all she could do to keep up with him.

He ran up the stairs and flung open the door without waiting for her. By the time Emily made it inside he had already thrown his raincoat on the kitchen floor and was kneeling beside Bertha.

"Vaseline," Keith shouted.

"I don't have any."

"Well, get something," he ordered.

She thought a moment and brought him a bottle of vegetable oil which he smeared on his hand. With the other hand he stroked the dog while he made soothing sounds. Emily sat down to watch. The dog strained and cried. Keith murmured and inserted a finger into the dog. Then he began urging, "Come on, Bertha," in exactly the same tone he would have used to encourage a horse in the home stretch.

Emily jumped to her feet as one pup and then another appeared in Keith's large hand. One was completely encased in its sac. Emily grabbed it, opened the sac, examined the pup and swung him until he let out a little cry. The other perfectly formed pup was stillborn.

Keith examined Bertha gently, then picked her up in his arms and staggered to the door with her. Emily held the door open and then quickly put clean papers in the box. Keith returned with the dog, laid her in the box, and put the four puppies to her nipples. Finally he switched off the light so that only the first light of dawn filtered through the window. He picked up the placenta pail and, with Job at his heels, went out. It had stopped raining.

Emily stood at the window and watched Keith walk across the muddy yard and into the woods. He had been in her house for almost an hour, during which time he had spoken to Bertha and Job and cooed at the puppies. To her, he had spoken exactly four words: *Vaseline, well, get* and *something.* But he had saved Bertha!

She stood with her head pressed against the cool glass wondering if she would see him again, marveling at his competence, thrilling at the mere thought of him. So now he was back at his camp. She closed her eyes, too weary to go to bed.

The sound of raucous singing pierced the silence. "How much is that doggie in the window?" Keith strode toward the house, swinging the bucket with Job running and yipping beside him. Without knocking, he entered the kitchen.

"Let's celebrate," he said, opening her refrigerator and pulling out a bottle of orange juice. He pushed Emily into a chair, rummaged in her cupboards until he found two glasses, and poured the juice. "To motherhood," he said, tapping his glass to hers.

They sipped in comfortable silence, and then he got to his feet and began to make breakfast. Emily tried to rise but he pushed her back in her chair. In an amazingly short time he brought plates of bacon, eggs, and toast to the table.

"I misjudged you," he said softly when he had finished his breakfast. "Where'd you learn about whelping?"

"From a book."

99

"Ever see a birthing before?" She shook her head. "You performed magnificently. I don't know what I expected when I got here, but it wasn't three perfect puppies sleeping peacefully. Did you have to revive any of them?"

"Just the first one. Job did the licking. What happened to the last two?"

"They entered the birth canal together. The first one was dead. I just manipulated them apart to they could be born one at a time. It was amazing the way you grabbed the live pup and got it started. What a midwife!" He grinned mischievously and, tired as she was, she felt a unnerving warmth flood her body.

He stood, took her hands, and raised her from her chair. She lifted her face and saw that he was looking right over her head. He wasn't even thinking of kissing her. With his arm around her he guided her toward the pantry where they, with Job beside them, stood watching a sleeping Bertha and three contented pups. The fourth one, the smallest and the last to be born, was scooting around on his fat tummy. Keith picked him up.

"Looks just like his father, doesn't he?" Emily murmured.

"He does indeed. Two of them do. You're a sly one, Job," Keith laughed, putting the puppy to a nipple. "And you, my dear little midwife, are about to fall asleep on your feet." He picked her up in his strong arms and carried her to her bed.

Emily awoke in a contented haze. She had been dreaming of puppies and a bearded man who looked like a beaver. Suddenly she sat up with a start, her mind panicking. Keith had laid her on her bed and kissed her—and then? She sat up and looked at herself. She was still wearing her shorts and T-shirt, disheveled though they were. She relaxed. He had kissed her gently and she had slipped into exhausted sleep.

The sun was streaming in the window. It was almost noon. She jumped up and ran to the pantry, where a bright-eyed Bertha lay with her pups.

"Good work, mother. Do you remember when Keith was here? He helped you when I thought you were lost. I'm sorry about the one pup, but you have four beautiful children."

Bertha turned her head and raised her nose as if to say, "I know." Then she got to her feet and walked steadily to the door.

The dirty dishes which Emily knew she had left on the table were sparkling on the drain board. The table was wiped clean, and the book, turned to the chapter entitled "After Whelping," lay in the center of it. Tucked under the book was a note:

> Good morning—or is it afternoon?
> I put an egg and a piece of bread in Bertha's bowl before I left. Your book seems very thorough, but I don't believe it will be necessary to take either Bertha or the pups to the vet unless they develop problems. They look healthy to me. I'm taking Job to my camp as he seems almost too eager to lick his progeny. Please be ready at five for an evening of celebration which will include beaver watching—if you think your pets are cute, wait till you see mine.
>
> With admiration,
The assistant midwife
>
> P.S. I am weak in the spoken word department so let me write my apologies for the nasty things I said and thought. You shone last night. Peter would have been proud of you.

Emily sat and hugged herself, smiling. *You silly adolescent,* she said to herself. Finally, she roused herself, got organized, and headed for the laundromat. While her clothes were in the dryer, she dropped in to see Josie Peck. Hilda Gilbert was there and the three of them sipped minted iced tea and discussed the great success of the weekend, the welcome rain which had held off just long enough, and the birth of the pups.

"What will you name them?" Josie asked.

"Don't name them," Hilda warned. "If you do, it will be just that much harder to dispose of them."

"Dispose?" Emily was shocked. "I'll find homes for them. They're adorable. I won't have trouble finding people to take them. Besides, if they're like their father, they'll be very smart."

"And if they're like their mother?" asked Hilda.

"Then they won't be very bright but they'll be loving."

"I personally think that appropriate names are of the greatest importance," said Josie as she left the room and returned with her Bible. "Here we have it. The three daughters of Job were named Jemima, Kezia, and Kerren-happuch. 'And in all the land were no women found so fair as the daughters of Job: and their father gave them inheritance among their brethren.' How many females are there?"

"I don't know. Two of each, I think."

"I can't find the names of the sons of Job but his friends were Eliphaz, Bildad and Zophar—and then there was Elihu."

Keith arrived at exactly five o'clock and stood in the doorway smiling at her. "I wish you could have seen yourself last night. You looked like a waif; your hair was matted and your eyes drooped."

"A vision of loveliness."

"That's what you are tonight," he said softly. "A vision with a halo. I'll bet you always played the part of the angel in the Christmas pageant, didn't you?" Emily nodded and laughed. "Still there was something very appealing about you last night too." He kissed her lightly on the cheek.

The two went and stood over the dog box. Emily told him about the names Josie had found in the Bible. Keith picked up the first and largest pup. Already his face bore sagging creases like Job's.

"Elihu," Emily laughed. "Called Eli or Hugh." She reached for the last-born pup and the obvious runt. "That's my Billy," Emily said as she handed the squirming dog to Keith.

The other two looked alike, but not at all like their brothers. They were light brown. Keith said they were both female.

"So what will it be?" Keith asked. "I don't like Jemima. It sounds like pancakes."

Emily picked Kezia for the one with a white tip on her tail. The other was Keren-happuch, to be called Keren, Happy or Kappy. She snuggled each of them against her cheek and put them beside their mother.

She straightened up and looked into a smile that made her swallow and turn away. The atmosphere was so charged that Emily would not have been surprised to see bolts of lightning fly through the room. Keith took her arm and they walked out toward the pond. Along the way she began to laugh.

"A penny?" he questioned her.

"I was just thinking about how my Grandma Grace must be turning over in her grave. She raised me very carefully." Emily's tone was one of mock severity. "She would not have approved of my running for you in the middle of the night to preside at the birth of puppies." She shrugged her shoulders. "But perhaps she would have recognized it as an emergency. The vet was away. I couldn't get Bertha to the car to take her to the animal hospital. I had no other choice."

"You could have phoned Gil."

Emily turned and stared at him. "Why didn't I? I never even thought of the Gilberts, and I could have

103

phoned them instead of going out in the rain."

"I'm glad you didn't."

She wished he would not smile at her like that; it made her knees rubbery.

"Busy as beavers." Keith pointed to V-shaped patterns moving across the surface of the pond, with a brown head at the point of each V.

"Busy working or busy playing?"

Keith said they were working to repair damage caused during the storm the night before. He showed her the three large lodges, each the home of a pair of adult beavers, a pair of one-year-olds and a pair of newborns. Young beavers, he explained, lived at home until they were two years old. Then they either left voluntarily or their parents drove them out. The males started off on foot and in the water, leaving their scent to be followed by an eager female who would follow to an appropriate spot. There the two of them would build a dam if necessary and a lodge.

No human, he said, could build a water-tight dam using the same materials beavers use—logs, twigs, and mud. Having established their homes, they often live in them for life—about twenty years.

"They mate for life. They're not like humans who swear to love and honor one another till death and then run off as soon as the going gets tough or one of them sees someone who is more attractive or more amusing or wealthier." His tone was bitter. "I guess that's why I am so attracted to beavers."

Two baby beavers came on shore and began to tumble together.

"They're adorable," Emily whispered. "Not as cute as my puppies, of course. They have buck teeth."

The youngsters scampered back into the water.

"You hurt their feelings. Those buck teeth make it possible for them to gnaw trees. The teeth keep growing all their lives."

He led her toward his truck.

"Why don't we save gas and take my car," she suggested. She locked her house carefully with Job outside and handed Keith her car keys.

As they drove through town she waved to Wilbert Wilson who was shutting up his office, and to Nika who was standing in front of the gallery, and to Mrs. Chamberlain who was hurrying toward the parsonage with her guitar slung over her shoulder.

"You've really made a place for yourself here, haven't you?" he said. "I was sure you'd be frightened away by the broken window…"

"How'd you know about that?"

"I saw it. It was brave of you to stay after that." He reached for her hand, and they drove in silence until they pulled off the road into a parking lot and went into a huge barn-like structure decorated with old tools. Keith asked for the main diningroom, and as they entered it, Emily saw that the restaurant was perched right at the edge of a lovely lake. She gasped with delight.

"It's like a picture on a postcard," she whispered.

"I thought you'd like it."

They were seated at a table by the window. A clump of white birches surrounded by ferns separated them from the lake. It was not a fancy place, but it was enchanting. Everything on the salad bar was tasty and crisp. The scallops were tiny and sweet.

Keith had written that he was not good with the spoken word, but Emily found his conversation fascinating. He talked about how beavers change their environment and about the work he was doing. He talked briefly about his classes at Williams and the changes wrought by coeducation. They debated the advantages of single-sex and coeducational colleges. It was casual, but at the same time intimate. Emily had never met a man so attractive in her entire life.

He pulled her close to him for the ride home and then came in with her to admire the pups. They let

Bertha out for her evening stroll. The dog who had been close to death just hours earlier seemed completely recovered and quite pleased with herself and her pups.

Emily and Keith took glasses of iced tea out to the back porch and sat on the steps with his arm draped over her shoulder. They sat sipping in silence until suddenly he put his glass down. He pulled her closer into his arms.

"Oh, Em," he breathed, pressing her to his chest, kissing her hair.

She raised her face and he brought his mouth down on hers. She had no strength—no wish—to resist. She heard a *boom*. *Another storm,* she thought, clinging to Keith. He pushed her aside and started running toward the pond.

"Call the fire department!" he shouted as he ran.

Emily looked around bewildered. Flames were shooting into the air between the pond and the road. She ran to the phone.

After she had called, she and Job hurried together to the pond. With the first wail of the fire siren, she felt reassured. Keith was in the pond throwing buckets of water onto the flaming dam.

The firemen arrived and completed the job with a long blast of their hose. Then they stood around uncertainly until someone started searching the ashes with a floodlight and a rake. Eddy, who was one of the volunteers, came and stood by her. Keith was walking back and forth in the water.

"It was dynamite all right," the chief announced for all to hear. "Who would dynamite the beaver dam? Why? We know some people have said things about..." He and all the other firemen turned to Emily.

Eddy put his arm around her protectively, daring the chief to go on.

Keith took one look at her and then continued to

scan the pond. Finally he waded out with a bundle of matted brown fur, which he laid on the ground.

"One of the yearlings," he said angrily.

While she stood on the shore, Emily became aware of activity in the pond. Beavers were swimming toward the dam, branches clenched in their teeth. Everyone stopped talking to watch the beavers working by moonlight.

"Thanks," Keith said to the firemen. "It will take more than a stick of dynamite to deter these creatures. They'll have their dam rebuilt in no time. I doubt that the underwater structure was damaged much anyway."

The firemen turned and walked silently to their trucks and cars. Keith picked up the dead beaver and started toward his camp. Emily and Job followed.

"Please go home," he said without turning around. His voice was infinitely tired and sad.

As she lay awake in her bed, Emily tried to sort her thoughts and emotions. In fewer than twenty-four hours she had seen so many facets of this man. There was the competent man who had known what to do for Bertha. There was the gentle man who had fed her and laid her exhausted body on her bed and then cleaned up the kitchen. There was the wounded, bitter man who had referred to the faithlessness of women.

She stopped to wonder if he had been married. *Probably. He must be in his early thirties. It couldn't have been a happy marriage.* She thought then of the sad man who had held the dead beaver in his arms. Finally she thought of the passionate man who had kissed her and held her close.

Is this love? she asked herself.

She knew the answer. She was deeply in love with Keith Cavanaugh.

Chapter Seven

Buddy arrived the next morning with a pair of slatted rockers. *Nice for the verandah,* Emily thought, *once I've scrubbed off ages of grime.* She invited him to leave them outside and come in to see the puppies. His ugly face, as he stared down into the box, was a study in awe.

"Pretty," he whispered, reaching down to them. Then he straightened up and clenched his hands together. "Don't touch."

"Not yet," Emily said. "When they're a little bigger you can come and play with them. Do you have a dog, Buddy?"

"Dead. Named Spot. Old and dead. Long time ago." Tears trickled down the boy-man's cheeks.

"Would you like one of these puppies, Buddy?"

A smile split his face. "I buy," he said eagerly, handing her one of the bills she had just given to him. "I buy."

"You talk with your sister about it." She forced the bill back in his hand. "They can't leave their mother yet."

Buddy studied the puppies carefully. One little ball of fur groped toward the edge of the box and seemed to look into Buddy's face.

"That one," he said eagerly. "I buy that one."

"If that's the one you want. Later you can look them all over and then decide. Her name is Kappy. She's a girl dog."

"Bye, bye, Kappy," he crooned. "Buddy be back."

Emily watched him drive off in his smelly truck and felt a glow of happiness. Kappy was going to look like her mother. If she were loving like Bertha, she'd be a perfect choice for Buddy.

She ran a comb through her curls, tucked her mint-green T-shirt into her matching shorts, and ran across the yard toward the beaver pond. Feeling a little shy, she decided to postpone meeting Keith and turned away from the path to his camp to check the dam. The beavers had been busy during the night. A little water trickled over the top in one spot, but the structure was essentially watertight. She heard footsteps in the brush, and Keith emerged on the other side of the dam. He stopped when he saw her.

"Your beavers really put in a hard night of work, didn't they?" she called.

"Yes." His answer was short and stern.

Emily started down into the stream bed on the dry side of the dam to cross over to him.

"Stay there." He barked the command.

She stopped and stared at him, then shrugged her shoulders. "I'm sorry about the dam. I had such a good time last night—before the explosion. I thought maybe we…"

"*We* will do nothing. Go home." His blue eyes flashed. He turned and marched back into the brush.

Confused and hurt, Emily watched him until he disappeared, then she turned back toward her house. Who was this crank, ordering her about as if she were a dog?

She filled a pail with hot sudsy water, found a brush, and scrubbed the chairs Buddy had brought vigorously, angrily. What kind of man was Keith anyway? One hour he was tender and loving, the next he was harsh and brutal. Whatever his problem, he was too changeable. When the last bit of grime had been washed away from the chairs, she left them in the sun to dry. Then she attacked her living quarters with the same vigor.

In the afternoon, Tommy came to mow the lawn, bringing her a box of strawberries and an assortment of green vegetables. Still Emily found herself brooding over the zoologist with the nasty temper. Mingled with her anger with Keith was fear of the unknown person who had maliciously dynamited the beaver dam. The broken window could have been an accident or a prank; the attempt to destroy the dam was neither. The fire chief had alluded to the gossip about her.

After dinner Emily sat on her verandah swinging gently while Job slept a few feet away. The more she tried to put her thoughts in order, the more jumbled they became. A very small part of her wanted to defy the gossips, to assert her right to Peter Darrow's property, to prove that she could not be deterred by rocks and dynamite. The rest of her wanted to flee, to run for shelter. But where would she go?

Her reverie was interrupted by the sight of Eddy, waving as he walked down the lane. She ran to welcome him, feeling a surge of gratitude for this calm, even-tempered young man.

"Terrible night last night," he said. "My mother always bought me ice cream when she wanted to cheer me, so here's a quart. I hope you like chocolate chip."

"It's my favorite and you're a dear, but not everything is terrible. Come see what the stork brought, and my new chairs."

Eddy looked at the chairs first, then the pups. Before they returned to the swing with their bowls of ice cream, he drove a few nails into the rockers and announced that with a coat of paint they'd be as good as new.

"I'm worried about you," Eddy said when he had

finished his ice cream. "It looks like someone really has it in for you."

"The rock was just an accident or a prank." Emily tried to sound positive.

"And the dynamite?"

"Maybe someone doesn't like beavers."

"Maybe." Eddy did not sound convinced. "Were you home last night?"

Emily shook her head and then answered the question Eddy did not ask. "I went out to dinner with the professor."

"Maybe he set the dynamite. Professors do nutty things and call it research. Maybe he wanted to see how long it would take the beavers to rebuild."

"He wouldn't have killed one of his beavers. Besides, we were sitting on the back porch—talking—when the explosion took place." She felt herself blushing as she remembered what the explosion had really interrupted. She was glad Eddy could not see her in the dark.

"So that lets him off."

Eddy came the next night, too, and Saturday after work they went to Great Barrington for pizza. Emily did not see Keith, but she could not get him out of her thoughts.

Every day the puppies grew bigger and more demanding. Emily felt as if she were always changing the newspapers in their box or preparing food for Bertha. Hugh grew more like his father daily, and she hoped he would develop Job's personality. Kezia and Kappy were bigger than their brothers and more placid. Billy was the ugliest, the smallest, the most spirited—and Emily's favorite.

The following week Emily had a call from a Mrs. Cook who said she was a friend of a friend of Nika's. She loved Victorian houses and she hoped that she and her husband could rent a room in her house for two weeks at the end of July. They had friends who wanted to rent another room for one week and two weekends. They required beds, a bridge table, and a light breakfast, nothing more. She knew that the house was not completely furnished, but said it didn't matter.

Flustered by the unexpected call, Emily agreed to call back the next day with her answer. Then she went for advice.

"How lucky for you," Ruth Gilbert said excitedly. She offered to lend her blankets, pillows, and a couple of lamps. Breakfast would be no problem, she assured Emily. She could set up a table with her toaster and coffee pot so that the guests could serve themselves when they were ready. She could use paper plates and napkins. The raspberries would be ripe and the Gilberts would keep her supplied. What could be more impressive than a big bowl of raspberries and a pitcher of cream on the breakfast table?

Eddy and Mr. Riley agreed with Ruth Gilbert. Eddy came that night to turn on the water in the upstairs bathrooms and to repair the one small leak. He told her she could get beds at the auction barn and he'd help her paint.

Emily called Mrs. Cook and told her the front room would be forty dollars a night, the back room would be thirty-five—and she began to worry the minute the woman accepted.

The owner of the auction barn sold her a cot with a mattress and three double-bed mattresses and springs, all in fairly good condition. He also delivered a miserable chest of drawers, a desk with a missing leg, and a sturdy but scarred bridge table. She had agreed to pay one hundred and twenty-five dollars from the first money she received from her guests.

She went to a discount store and bought shades for the windows, sheets and towels, and four folding chairs. Then she went to the fabric mill and bought more cheap white cotton for curtains and fabric for spreads.

Eddy sent an electrician to work on the wiring and came himself every night to help. He made a new leg for the desk, screwed legs into all of the box springs, and then helped her paint. Emily put in sixteen-hour days, grateful for the exhausting labor that helped her keep her mind off Keith Cavanaugh.

Bertha was beginning to make her own life easier; she was weaning the puppies.

"When are you going to start toilet training them?" Emily asked impatiently.

On the Friday the Cooks were due to arrive, Emily was up early. After a hasty breakfast, she went upstairs to make the beds and put on the finishing touches, beginning with the bedroom over the library.

The floors and woodwork glowed golden brown in the morning sunshine. The walls had been painted with left-over blue from her sitting room mixed with left-over green from the front bedroom. The furniture was painted white, and the shades and cafe curtains were also white. The spreads for the double bed and the cot were a floral design. Above the bed was a large floral print on loan from the gallery, a small price tag in the corner—Nika's idea. Someone might fall in love with the picture and buy it. *An attractive room,* Emily thought, as she pulled the shades to cut the glare.

Her pride, however, was the octagonal front bedroom. It was a lovely room empty and looked even more inviting now. The pale green walls set off the antiqued dressing table and chest of drawers. The two double beds sat side-by-side with a little wicker table from her sitting room between them. The spreads were an open green-on-white print with touches of shocking pink.

She checked the cedar-lined closet to see that there were enough hangers. When the Cooks had gone she would take time to remove all the hooks, which Eddy said were solid brass and could be cleaned to their original splendor. *Such graceful hooks,* she thought, grabbing the one to the left of the door. It needed tightening. As she tried to screw it into the wall, the whole wall swung open, like a door, on concealed hinges.

And there it was! The safe, imbedded in the cement of the fireplace, just above the floor level of the closet. A book was sitting on a cement ledge above the safe. She squatted down to examine the big, black iron box. It had been locked with a key. Checking her watch, she picked up the book, closed the concealed door, and latched it with a turn of the hook.

Oh, you were a clever man, Peter Darrow, she said to herself. She laid the small thick book, bound in green cloth, carefully on her kitchen table and opened it. The pages were lined and the writing was neat and clear—a steadier version of the handwriting she knew to be Peter Darrow's.

Emily closed the book reluctantly and placed it in the drawer of her bedside table on top of Peter's Bible. Then she checked the dogs, locked the doors, and drove to work filled with the excitement of discovery, wishing she had someone with whom to share her excitement. Maybe she would tell Eddy. When the Cooks had left she would tell the lawyer and the executors so that the safe could be opened and the deed removed.

"Hi there, Emily." Nika called as she entered the shop. Then she gave her a searching look. "You look like the cat who swallowed the canary. What's the news?"

"I'm all ready for my guests." Funny, Emily thought, a few minutes ago she had been wishing to share her discovery; now she wanted to conceal it. "You have to come see the Briggs watercolor over the fireplace, Nika. It makes the room. I'd almost hate to sell it."

"You sell it and we'll find something else just as suitable. We have plenty of paintings to choose from."

Nika left to sketch an old house that had just been restored by summer people.

Emily was quaking when she heard the two cars in her driveway. Job, locked in the kitchen, was barking furiously. What if her guests were demanding and disagreeable or allergic to dogs? What if they didn't like their rooms? What if...

She straightened her spine, switched on the verandah light, and took a deep breath. Grandma Grace would be charming in this situation. Emily ran her fingers through her hair to fluff it and walked briskly out onto the verandah to meet her guests.

"How nice of you to come," she said as she extended her hand, realizing with a shock that she sounded just like Grace. "Are you very tired after your long drive? Do come in and I'll show you your rooms. Then perhaps you'd like to relax for a while on the verandah." Did she sound phony? Probably, but it was better than her usual shy stammer.

They greeted her pleasantly and followed her inside. The woman who had introduced herself as Mrs. Cook stopped in the doorway.

"Magnificent," she breathed, then stepped aside so that the others could come inside too.

The last rays of light penetrated the stained glass so that muted colors bathed the stairway and marble floor. Emily had left a single light burning in each of the bedrooms, and her guests were genuinely delighted with the rooms. She showed them the bathrooms and indicated the bridge table and chairs leaning against a wall in the hall.

They continued to express their satisfaction when they returned to the verandah. She explained that breakfast would be set up in the sitting room whenever they wanted it and gave them keys to the front door so they could come and go as they pleased. Then she brought Job, Bertha, and Kezia out to meet them.

She promised to keep Job on the chain when she was at work. Bertha and the pups would be locked in her private quarters. Then Emily said good night and took the dogs back to the kitchen. In bed, she reached eagerly for Peter's journal.

Chapter Eight

April 25, 1928.

Today it was finally dry enough to clear the land for our house. I wish you had been here. We could have had a little ceremony. But, of course, I am glad you are in Boston enjoying the concerts and museums. Did you know that we call April the mud month? Fortunately for you and me, this April is dryer than most. I hated to fell the old oak. It had been a beacon on the property for as long as I can remember. I confess that at the last minute I looked around for another place for the house, but you and I chose this spot and it is perfect. After the land was cleared and the men had gone, I stayed behind and said a prayer. I thanked God for guiding you from North Carolina to your uncle at the parsonage here—and to me. I asked Him to bless our house. We shall be so happy!

May 8.

Rain, rain, rain. I long to get the cellar dug and the house started, but I have not wasted these wet weeks. I have ordered the marble for the hall floor. I'm sorry if I seemed miserly when you first suggested it. It was just that I had not pictured anything so grand. But I want you to have whatever you want. I also ordered a stained-glass window. I love to picture you standing on the landing with the light streaming through the window adding to the glow of your halo. It will be like the first time I saw you—in church with the sun shining through the window.

June 12.
At last the hole is dug and the concrete is poured. It looks enormous! Of course I was disappointed—actually heartbroken—that you could not come back to Stonefield before going on to Cape Cod, but when you come in the fall there will be a real house with walls and roof to show you. I saw the beaver kittens for the first time last week. Did you know that beavers mate for life? So will I. There will be only one woman in my life for as long as I live.

July 14.
The skeletal walls are up and part of the roof. I stood back and looked at it and wondered why on earth we were building such a mansion. And then I thought about all of the friends you write about on the Cape, and your dear mother—how I long to meet her—in the South. They will all visit us here and you will be so proud to entertain them. And then there will be babies. A little girl who will look just like you, and a boy—maybe several boys. I will buy a telescope so they can watch the beavers from the tower room. They will love sliding down the banister.

August 21.
Work was held up when my mother died suddenly. She went as she would have wished, suddenly and without warning. I am glad she could see the house—or at least its outlines—before she died. She has had so many disappointments in her own life that it was hard for her to believe that something will not destroy my happiness. Poor Mother! I wish you had been able to attend her funeral, but I know how tiring the train trip

would have been. It was inconsiderate of me to ask you to come.

September 26.
Three glorious weeks with you here in Stonefield! You did like the house, didn't you? Of course it still takes a lot to imagine how it will be. But the fireplaces are nice, aren't they? The safe arrived. Ed Riley laughed when he saw the size of it. He does not know, nor did I tell him, of my plans to buy you jewels to put in the safe. He helped me install it, but even he, my best friend, does not know about the latching hook and the secret panel. That will delight your romantic heart. I put something in there for you already. I wish we could have married at Christmas, but you are right; we should begin our married life in our new home. It will be ready for you to select the wallpaper and paint when you return in the spring. We can surely marry this summer. I'm glad you liked the maid's room and bath. I thought I had written to you about my decision to add them on behind the kitchen. Surely you did not think that I would expect you to keep up this big house all by yourself.

December 25.
Next Christmas we will have a Christmas tree in the parlor, and I will hang garlands of greenery all along the main staircase. Those dreams sustain me during this dreary season, the first Christmas since my mother's death. I wish I knew more about the stockbroker who is visiting in North Carolina. He makes me uneasy. Jealousy, I guess. I had Christmas dinner with the parson. Josie Peck was there. Do you remember her? I hope you and she will be great friends. I have known her all my life. She teaches here and is the kind of cultured person who will make you feel less isolated in Stonefield. Josie asked about the house, but since you have wanted our engagement to be kept secret, I did

not tell her that it is your house.

February 14.
Valentine's Day and I did not hear from Grace. The house is all but finished. The stairway is magnificent. I was lucky to have found such a craftsman. The window is all I hoped for. Grace was right about the marble floor. It was worth every penny. I would like to paint and paper the rooms this spring—and buy furniture—but I will wait to hear from Grace. Perhaps I should get on a train and go visit her. I suggested that but I have not heard from her.

May 14.
All five peonies I planted last fall are peeking through the soil and give me renewed hope. Grace has written so seldom since Christmas and her letters have been so brief—quite unlike the wonderful letters she wrote earlier. She says she is going to Boston before coming here. The stockbroker lives in Boston. The house is done. It is even paid for and I have enough to buy furniture and decorations. It is a magnificent house. If only Grace would come see it before she goes to Boston! Surely she could not resist it—and my love.

Chapter Nine

The rest of the pages were blank, but there was an envelope stuck between the first blank pages. Emily opened it with a sense of dread. Poor Peter! He had built his house with such love and...

June 16, 1929

My dear Peter,

When you receive this letter, I will be an old married lady. Thadeus Potter and I will marry tomorrow. We will honeymoon in Virginia and Washington, D.C., and then head for Boston. I shall mail this letter from there.

Of course I should have told you sooner, but you are so unpredictable that I couldn't be sure what you would do. I have written to you from time to time about Thadeus, so I hope our marriage will not come as too great a surprise. He is a very wealthy stockbroker—a Harvard graduate who loves the symphony and art and parties.

Some people say I am flighty but what girl could exchange an apartment on Beacon Hill for a funny brown house with only beavers for company? I know you will be happy for me and that you will find someone else to share your house.

Emily put her grandmother's letter back in the envelope. She switched off the light and lay with her head propped up on her hands, thinking, feeling Peter Darrow's pain of long ago.

The mystery was solved. Peter Darrow had built this house with joy and love for the girl who had become Emily's grandmother. Grace had said that when she was young she had come north for an extended visit with her mother's brother, a clergyman. What Emily had not known was that the clergyman lived in Stonefield. Peter Darrow had fallen in love with the Southern belle and asked her to marry him.

And Grace? Scheming Grace had led him on— until Thadeus Potter with his Harvard education and his greater wealth had come along. *Scheming* was too cruel. Grace was not a schemer. She was just a vain, silly woman who somehow managed to float with the most favorable breeze. Grandpa Potter had adored her.

She had married Grandpa in June of 1929. Within six months the stock market had crashed. That must have come as a personal insult to Grace, but Grandpa protected her from the worst of it. Had that woman ever once faced a harsh reality? Emily felt a surge of anger and then she laughed. Why should she? She had been pretty and charming and men had been happy making her happy.

It was a successful strategy that had served Grace well all her life. And she had not been selfish with her strategy; she had done her best to pass it on to her granddaughter. She had probably tried to give it to her daughter too, but Emily's mother had rebelled. She had married a "foreigner" and exchanged her frilly dresses for jeans and marched in peace demonstrations.

Undeterred by her experience with her own daughter, Grace had thrown away her granddaughter's jeans and bought her pretty dresses and educated her to be a useless parasite. *What an apt pupil I was,* Emily thought ruefully.

At least she now knew why she had inherited this house. Peter had said that there would be only one woman in his life as long as he lived. Grace Gresham had been the single love of his life. He had built a house for her, and when he was old and dying he had willed the house to Grace's only descendant. At his funeral he had requested one hymn, "Amazing Grace."

Poor Peter! She had come to believe that she was his grandchild. She was not. His love for Grace had been sterile: *unrequited* was the old-fashioned term.

Before she fell asleep she asked herself another question: What if she had not looked like Grace? Would Peter have left this house to her if she had been dark like her father? If he had not left it to her, then who would have inherited it?

Fortunately for Emily, her guests left early the next morning to attend the rehearsal at Tanglewood. Before they left they raved about the raspberries and cream, applauded her coffee, and begged her not to serve sweet rolls in the future. They would prefer plain toast.

As soon as they had driven away, she ran upstairs to clean their rooms and bathrooms and to put clean sheets on the beds. She tended to the dogs and left for work, dropping the linen at the Laudromat.

It was the ideal summer day—hot, but with a fresh, cool breeze. Steady streams of tourists flooded the gallery, buyers as well as lookers. Emily was making change for the purchase of four woodcuts when there was a commotion at the doorway. She looked up to see two young girls. One was the short, stocky child she had seen in the lumberyard the day Eddy had been invited to a party. The other was thin and leggy with a head of glaring orange-colored curls.

"See it's not the same at all. You shouldn't have let me do it." She burst into tears and ran out.

The stocky one looked at Emily, shrugged her shoulders, and ran after her friend. A bewildered Emily went on to the next customer, dragging out every floral silk screen in the gallery and finally putting them all away when the potential customer announced, in a loud voice, that they were all over-priced.

"Sorry about that," Nika sympathized during a brief break while Emily was still stacking the prints. "You can't please all the people, but you'd think they could decide the prints were too expensive *before* they made you drag out every single one. By the way, who's the kid who wants to look like you? Poor little goose!"

"Look like me?" Emily was stunned. "She used to have lovely, long chestnut hair. Why would she do that to herself?" Emily leaned across the counter and looked directly into Nika's face. "Tell me the truth. Does my hair look like that?"

Nika ruffled her curls. "It does not." She began to guffaw. "Imagine that child going to the local beauty parlor and saying, 'I want to look just like Emily Stanoszek.' I hope the hair dresser made an effort to dissuade her before she got out the scissors, permanent wave lotion, bleach, and dye. Some fix the kid's in now." Nika's guffaw turned into a belly laugh so that she could hardly catch her breath and waddle over to the next customer.

Emily felt only pity, remembering when she had admired a girl in boarding school with lovely black hair. Emily had gone out to buy a wig, but her roommate had laughed so hard at the sight of Emily in long black hair that she had not made the purchase. She had, however, let her hair grow for months until it was long and stringy. When her grandmother had seen it she made an appointment to have her hair cut that very day.

Late in the afternoon Wilbert Wilson sauntered in, looked briefly at the pictures, and then spoke to Emily. "Found the deed yet?"

"No. But I've found the safe. I'll have to figure out a way to open it when my guests leave."

"Guests? Oh, of course, friends from Boston. Why do they have to leave before you open the safe?"

"Not friends. Paying guests. I've rented two rooms."

"You've..." The lawyer flushed. "I hope you have insurance. A fall on the stairway, a bite from one of the dogs, and you'd be ruined."

"I went to the insurance man Mr. Riley suggested. I'm covered."

"Well, when you get ready to open the safe, give me a call. I really must be there when you open it. To protect you, my dear."

"Of course. I suppose Mr. Yost and Mr Chamberlain should come too. We can have a safe-opening party."

"How is everything else? I hear there was a fire at the beaver dam. Who do you think started it? Buddy? The professor? The professor is not molesting you, I hope."

"Molesting me!" she exclaimed in astonishment. He wasn't even speaking to her.

127

"We really know so little about him. We do know Buddy. He's very strong, if simple-minded. Just keep your doors locked." The lawyer sauntered out, leaving Emily to stare after him.

That evening she unleashed an unhappy Job and went out on the verandah where her guests were playing bridge in the fading twilight. They'd had a wonderful day—the rehearsal, a late lunch, a stroll through Stockbridge, and a visit to the Norman Rockwell museum. They were going to the restaurant in Stonefield for dinner when they finished the rubber. Emily fell into bed, exhausted.

When she arrived home from the gallery on Sunday night her guests had already had dinner and were watching the beavers cavort in the pond before they went upstairs for more bridge.

Couldn't be an easier way to make money, Emily thought as she drifted off to sleep.

The next morning she dragged herself from bed, set out breakfast, let the dogs out, and went back to bed. The weekend was over; she could take things easier today since she did not have to go to the gallery.

It seemed that she had just closed her eyes when she heard a banging on the pantry door and the puppies began to yip. She staggered from bed, wrapped her robe around her, and opened the door.

"Yes?" she yawned.

"Sorry to bother you, Emily," Mr. Cook said, "But there's no water in either of the bathrooms." He sipped his coffee. "Boy, those blueberries look good. You spread a great table."

"No water!" She was instantly awake. "How could there be no water? There was water for the coffee." She ran back to the kitchen and turned on the faucet. There was a tiny spurt and then nothing.

"Don't worry. These things happen. We'll manage." Mr. Cook reached down to pat the puppies. "Cute little fellows."

Emily ran to the phone and called Eddy, explaining her predicament in a few disjointed sentences. She felt reassured when he promised to come immediately. He was driving into the lane by the time she had changed into yellow shorts and a white T-shirt and sneakers. She wished she could brush her teeth; her mouth felt stuffed with cotton. Instead she poured herself a mug of coffee and went out to meet him. He went to the basement and was back in her kitchen within minutes.

"There's no water coming into the house." He pushed his shock of blond hair off his forehead. "I don't understand it. My dad says that it's a wonderful spring. It's never gone dry. There must be a problem in the line, but we replaced all of that not long ago. Want to come with me to check it?"

Emily tagged along into the woods between her house and the Gilberts. The pipe ran under ground. Deep in the woods, where Emily had never been before, a sloped shingled roof sat hidden in the bushes. Eddy opened the door at one end and peered in with the aid of his flashlight. Then he pushed Emily in front of him and directed her gaze to a pipe at the edge of a full water tank. There were holes in the pipe so that water poured back into the open tank.

"I wonder how you'd get holes in the middle of a pipe," she said, baffled. "It looks like it's in good shape otherwise. Could an animal bite into pipe and make those holes with its teeth?"

"Only a human animal with a chisel and hammer," he replied angrily. "I'll replace the pipe later today. In the meantime I'll tape it so that you'll have water in the house right away." Eddy took a roll of tape out of his pocket and began work.

"You come equipped for every emergency," Emily said when he was finished. "I'm grateful, Eddy, really grateful. I don't think I could manage here without you."

He looked at her for a long time. "I'll fix the pipe tonight and then I'll take you out for a steak. Okay?"

"No, I'll take you out for a steak," Emily laughed.

"I will take you." His tone allowed no argument on the subject.

As soon as he had driven off, she ran into the house to tell her guests that the crisis was over. They seemed not in the least concerned as they lounged on the verandah, sipping coffee. They told her their plan to drive to Vermont for the day, stopping at the Grandma Moses museum in Bennington. They would not be back until after dinner.

Eddy took her to a pleasant little steak house with checked tablecloths and candles. Watching him down a huge steak, Emily thought he ate like a boy, and then remembered he was barely beyond boyhood.

She told him about Peter Darrow's journal, but he seemed far away and scarcely listening to her. Toward the end of the meal she reached across the small table and took his hand.

"Is something the matter?" she asked. "You seem preoccupied."

In answer he stood up, checked the bill, dropped money on the table, and ushered her out. She hadn't even finished her coffee. He drove home in silence.

"Have I offended you?" she asked anxiously.

130

"No." He offered no explanation.

When he stopped his car in her driveway, she reached for the door handle and was about to invite him in for coffee when he grabbed her hand away from the door. "Stay here," he commanded. "You've got to marry me."

Emily was speechless. All her school-girl dreams had never prepared her for a proposal like this one. Actually it was not a proposal but a statement of fact, a command. Why did she have to marry him?

"I know I'm not good enough for you.... you've graduated from that fancy college....like music I don't understand...have a big house worth a lot of money..."

"Stop, Eddy. You're being silly. You are good enough for me or any other woman. You can do all kinds of things that baffle me. You are good and kind and capable."

"Does that mean you'll marry me?" He looked at her for the first time all evening. He did not smile. "Right away? As soon as we can get a license or whatever it is we need."

"Why?"

"You're not safe. The window...the dam...the pipe...the gossip. It would stop if I were here. Besides, you need someone to keep this big house going. Insulation, paint, repairs. You told me tonight about how Peter Darrow, when he owned the lumberyard, built this house because he thought your grandmother was going to marry him. I'm going to own the lumberyard one day. It would be nice, don't you think?" He smiled for the first time. "I'm young but everyone says I'm mature for my age. What do you think?"

"I think you are very mature." Emily sat thinking about the lumberman and her grandmother and came to a quick and positive decision. She could not be like Grace and let this dear man think for even an instant that she had any intention of marrying him. "I can't marry you, Eddy, now or ever. You've been good to me and I've been thoughtless in asking you to do so much. I've probably kept you away from your old friends here in Stonefield." She thought of the leggy girl with the shocking orange curls who might have been Eddy's usual date before Emily came to town. "I won't monopolize your time any longer."

"But you're so helpless. You need a man," he insisted.

"I'm not helpless, Eddy. I simply have a character flaw. All my life I've depended on the kindness of strangers. Not any more." She hoped she sounded more convincing to him than she did to herself.

"But you need me," he repeated. "I do love you. You know that, don't you? I really love you." Somehow he was not convincing.

"Thank you, Eddy. I love you too in a gentle way, but not in the way I'll love the man I'll marry." She pushed the picture of herself with Keith out of her mind, knowing that the passion she had felt for him was what she wanted to feel for her husband. She opened the door and slid out.

Eddy followed her and was standing behind her as she let the dogs out. She was grateful to them both for their noisy greetings which made conversation impossible.

"Want to see the pups before you go?" she asked.

He followed her inside and she picked up Kappy and handed the round little pup to him. "She's already found a home with Buddy. He can take her in a couple of weeks, as soon as she's had

132

her shots." Emily picked up Billy and rubbed noses with him. "I think you're getting bigger," she said.

Eddy put Kappy back in the box. "Can't we talk about it some more?"

"No. There's nothing to talk about." Still holding Billy, she followed him to the door and kissed him lightly on the cheek. "Thank you for being such a good friend."

She watched him drive away, feeling lonely and grateful for Billy's warm little body against her neck. It was going to be difficult managing without Eddy. Just today she had thought about asking him to make a pen for the pups. It was time for them to begin spending time outside.

Emily moped for two days. Her marigolds needed weeding and she had no strength to tackle the job. The kitchen floor was dirty and she did not scrub it. She prepared breakfast for her guests, cleaned their rooms daily, and changed the sheets. She also took care of the pups who were being neglected by their mother now that they were weaned. Feeling too dejected even to cook, Emily lived on peanut butter sandwiches. Afternoons and evenings, she lay on her bed listening to the radio and reading novels she knew she would forget the following week.

One afternoon Ruth Gilbert stopped in with a basket of vegetables. Emily pretended a gratitude and enthusiasm she did not feel. Ruth chatted for a few minutes about how busy they had been, about the quality of the corn and the raccoon who was trying to beat them to the harvest. Emily hardly heard her.

"Are you all right?" Ruth asked, putting her head on Emily's forehead.

"Fine." She turned away. Ruth's simple question

had brought tears to her eyes.

"Can I help? Come to dinner," Ruth pleaded. "We're just having hamburgers."

Emily shook her head, unable to speak. Ruth patted her shoulder and left.

When she was gone, Emily put her head down on the kitchen table and cried. She had never been so lonely. In boarding school and college she had been surrounded by other girls. Even in Boston, she had had Allison. Now she didn't even have Eddy.

Something crawled over her bare foot, and she looked down into a little white squeezed-up face.

"Billy! How did you get out of the box? Your brother and sisters have never escaped and they're bigger than you are." She found herself smiling at the pup as he tried to make his way across the slick floor, slipping and falling onto his fat tummy. "I know," she said as she picked him up and cuddled him close. "You're smarter than they are, and more independent." As she stroked him, he reached out and licked her arm with his little pink tongue. "You want to know a secret?" she whispered. "I love you best."

Chapter Ten

The next morning, while she was cleaning up after breakfast, the phone rang.

"Emily? Josie Peck here. I hate to bother you, dear, but I have just noticed that my books are due today and I wondered if by any chance you were planning to go to the library."

Emily's first impulse was to say no, she'd rather spend another day moping. Then she pictured the little lady with her bowed legs and said she'd pick her up as soon as she had cleaned upstairs and taken the linen to the laundromat.

In the library parking lot she held the car door open for Josie. The old woman handed her a stack of books so she would have both hands free to hoist her tiny body out of the car. The top book fell to the ground and opened to reveal the date-due card. The book was not due for another week.

"You're a sly one, Josie Peck. Did the Gilberts put you up to this?"

"Nevermind about that." She patted Emily's hand. "If you're feeling a little blue, may I suggest Jane Austen? She always cheers me. 'It is a truth universally acknowledged, that a single man in possession of a good fortune, must be in want of a wife.' That's what we thought about Peter Darrow many years ago."

"The opening sentence of *Pride and Prejudice*." Emily grinned fondly at her companion and thought about the Gilberts with a surge of warmth. Such good people! "Thank you, Josie," she said affectionately.

Emily ushered Josie into the library where they went their separate ways. When they had both checked out their reading supply—Emily's included *Emma, Mansfield Park,* and a book about beavers—and were back in the oven-like car which had been sitting in the sun, Josie made a suggestion. Perhaps Emily would enjoy a visit to Herman Melville's house, right there in Pittsfield. From her purse she pulled a newspaper clipping which described the house and showed how to get to it. They stopped for lunch, then visited the house.

Instead of taking Josie home, Emily took her to her house. "I want you to meet the pups," she explained. She poured glasses of iced tea while her elderly friend sat on one of the kitchen chairs. Emily was about to invite her into the pantry when she noticed Josie looked tired. She brought Kezia and put her in her guest's lap.

"Well, aren't you the pretty one?" Josie purred.

Billy was scrambling for attention, but Emily gave him just a quick tickle and then brought out Hugh. "Hugh," she said, "meet the lady who named you." She put Hugh in Josie's lap and took Kezia.

"Elihu is a noble name. I hope it pleases you. I suppose we can forgive Emily for shortening it, but if you were my dog, I would use your entire name. I have never believed in nicknames. Not everyone agrees with me of course. The Gilberts insist on calling their son Tommy; I always call him Thomas. We need all the dignity we can muster," she lectured the puppy in a mock-serious tone.

Emily laughed. "So why do you let people call you Josie? That can't be your real name?"

"Unfortunately, it is. My father thought it was cute. I did everything in my power when I was young to

136

change it to Josephine, but no one took me seriously."

"I can think of one way for you to make sure that Elihu is known by his full name."

"Oh no, I couldn't. I haven't the strength to train him. I…"

"He'd be good company. I could keep him for you until he's trained and has had all his shots."

"Oh, I…"

"Think about it." Emily returned Kezia and brought out Kappy who opened one eye and then went back to sleep. "This is Keren-happuch. I'm sorry to report that her future master, Buddy, calls her Kappy."

"Buddy needs a dog," Josie said approvingly.

"And now, Miss Josephine, I wish you to meet Bildad." The puppy had escaped again and was tottering toward them. He looked at the guest, bared his little white teeth, and yipped. His fierce-dog pose was ruined when all four of his tiny legs slid in opposite directions and he fell on his fat tummy. Josie laughed as Emily picked the pup up to comfort him. "You're not ready to be a watchdog yet. But you'll be terrific when you're bigger. Brave and loyal like your father, and smart, too."

"And that is your dog, Emily."

"I can't keep him. I already have Job and Bertha."

"You will," she stated with calm confidence.

Emily took the older woman home and carried her books into her apartment for her. Josie's skin was whiter than usual and she walked very slowly.

Aware of the great effort Josie had made on her behalf, Emily hardly knew how to say thank you, so she simply kissed her cheek and told her, honestly, that she felt much better.

She had picked up the laundry and was walking toward the grocery store when, too late to cross to the other side of the street, she saw Jay LaRoux approaching.

"Hi there, cutie," he greeted her. "Ready to sell out?"

"No." She pushed her way around him and went on to the store where she bought a piece of fresh fish and a baking potato. It was time to snap out of the peanut butter routine.

Waiting for her laundry the next afternoon, Emily dropped in on Josie, who looked perky as ever.

"You were right about Jane Austen." That was all Emily said about her blues, but it seemed to satisfy Josie Peek.

"Did you ever find out for whom Peter built his house?"

Emily sat down and told her about the journal and its contents.

"I thought you looked like someone I had seen before." Josie beamed at her. "So it was the pastor's niece. I wonder why I never thought of that. Of course I was teaching some distance from here. I saw her two or three times and then she went away. Somehow I never connected her visit with Peter's house. Stupid of me—or deliberately blind. Oh well, that was long ago." Her faded blue eyes shone wistfully. "Would you let me read the journal, Emily?"

Emily hesitated, wondering if Peter's devotion to Grace would be painful to Josie.

Josie read her thoughts. "Don't worry about me. I did love Peter, but that was long ago. I have had a satisfying life with the pleasures far outweighing the disappointments. Peter was a stubborn young man who, once he had an idea, never gave it up. He went to his grave without relinquishing his love for your grandmother...Well, some good came of it. It brought you to Stonefield."

"I'll bring the journal to you tomorrow, but you should know that my grandmother was not worthy of his lifelong devotion. She was foolish and shallow."

"Was she still pretty when she was old?"

"Indeed. Soft and always feminine. Her hands, even when they were wrinkled and misshapen, felt like silk. Right to the end, men adored her. Her accountant let her run up debts at his expense."

"Don't be too critical, Emily. Where are your parents, by the way?"

"They died when I was six. My grandparents raised me."

"Were they good to you?"

"Yes. I wasn't always happy, but they did their best."

"No one is always happy. I'd say that they did an excellent job. You are a sensitive, generous, well-educated young woman."

"With the backbone of a butterfly," Emily added.

Sunday Emily began to feel more self-sufficient when the Cooks' friends came to breakfast with their checkbook in hand.

"First let me say that we have had a lovely week," said the wife. "The breakfasts have been delicious and the room is comfortable and pretty. I noticed that there's a price tag on the print over the bed. Does that mean it's for sale?"

"Yes, it is," Emily said, happy that she could make a sale for Nika.

"Your rates are reasonable, too. If you want the advice of a businessman, you'll add another ten dollars a day." The husband sat down and wrote a check for four hundred dollars for the room and the print. "Whatever you do, don't economize by cutting back on the fresh fruits. Those berries were just the thing to make your guests feel pampered."

"I'm glad you've had a pleasant vacation," Emily said warmly. "I've enjoyed knowing you."

"Oh, you'll see us again," laughed the wife. "We'll be back next year."

If I'm still here, Emily thought as she drove off to church.

On Monday Emily opened a checking account, depositing the check from her guests and her earnings from the gallery. She felt like a woman of means. When she had finished, Mr. Yost invited her to step into his office. Shutting the door behind her, he asked her to have a seat and took his place behind the desk. Then he peered at her over the top of his half-glasses. With difficulty, Emily kept her eyes away from the mole on his jaw.

"How are you making out?"

"Fine. I have a part-time job at the gallery, and I've decorated and rented two of the upstairs bedrooms."

"So I heard. We could settle the estate if we could find that deed."

She explained about finding the safe. "But I don't know where the key is and I can't disturb my guests. I had planned to ask your advice when they leave. That will be on Sunday."

"Have you told Wilson?"

"Only that I have found the safe and that it can not be opened while my guests are here."

"Good. Would you mind if we did nothing about the deed for now? My wife and I are leaving for Maine this afternoon. I will return on Labor Day and contact a locksmith. I wish to be present when the safe is opened. Do not, I repeat, do not allow anyone, not anyone, to open it until I can be present." He frowned at her. "I'll phone Reverend Chamberlain before I leave. If anything comes up, go to him. I trust him."

Mr. Yost seemed to be saying that he did not trust the lawyer. Could that be?

"Thank you. I'm afraid this estate has been a terrible bother to you."

"Not at all. I'm glad you are doing well. I hear you have just opened a checking account with a rather sizable deposit." The corners of his thin, bloodless lips turned up briefly.

The rest of the week was uneventful. The Cooks spent their mornings reading on the verandah. They usually drove off before lunch and didn't return until after dinner. Whenever she saw them, they assured her that they were enjoying a perfect, restful vacation. Emily found herself envying them their concerts and plays and long drives in the country.

She moved the dog box from the pantry to the back porch, so now the pups spent their days in the open air. Nights she put them in a smaller box with high sides all around so Billy could not escape.

She spent her evenings enjoying the gentle humor of Jane Austen. Sometimes thoughts of Keith Cavanaugh disturbed her peace of mind, but most of the time she felt content.

The Gilberts were beginning to complain about the lack of rain, and she noticed that the beaver pond had receded so that several feet of dried mud were visible all around the edges.

The Cooks left on Sunday, and Emily made another solid deposit in her bank account on Monday.

When she returned from town on Monday, the navy blue Cadillac was in her driveway. Both dogs were barking furiously at the lawyer they were' keeping trapped inside.

"These dogs are incorrigible, Emily," Wilbert Wilson said crossly as he got out of his car mopping his brow. "I do wish you'd get rid of them."

"Sorry. We've taken quite a shine to one another. Even Job has become my friend. I wouldn't get rid of them for anything. Besides, they make me feel safe."

"So be it. I'm glad you feel safe. I worry about you being so isolated here. Have your guests gone?" Emily nodded. "So let's see about the safe."

"I'm sorry. Mr. Yost says he must be present when

141

the safe is opened, and he's in Maine now. When he comes back, we'll call in a locksmith and have it opened."

"Nonsense. You and I can open it or call in a locksmith if necessary. I am, after all, Peter Darrow's lawyer. And yours too, I trust."

"Of course. But Mr. Yost was most definite in his instructions. He said he positively has to be here when the safe is opened."

"Yost is a suspicious stick." Wilbert Wilson laughed heartily. "Aren't you curious? There may be all kinds of interesting things in there. Jewels maybe. They'd be yours. Let's have at it."

"No. I can wait." His eager persistence made her feel uncomfortable.

"The safe must have been well concealed. Where is it? In one of the bedrooms?"

"Would you like a cup of coffee?" Emily offered, sidestepping his question.

While the coffee was brewing, the lawyer asked if he could see the renovated bedrooms, suggesting that he might be able to help her rent them in the future. He examined the rooms carefully. He ran his fingers around the molding over the fireplace, as if inspecting for dust. Emily held her breath while he examined the closet. He did not touch the hooks. He showed little interest in the decor. Emily took the coffee out to the verandah and was pouring when Calvin Chamberlain drove up. She went back for another cup.

"Ah, the executor of the estate," the lawyer greeted him. "Now that you are here, Miss Emily will show us the safe and we can get this business settled."

"No. I am one of the two executors and ignorant of all things legal. We'll wait until Mr. Yost returns and then open the safe." The young minister sounded very definite, and he did not waver as the lawyer exercised his powers of persuasion.

"I hear that the parsonage kitchen is quite inadequate," said Wilson slyly. "I could have it remodeled for you, but....I'd expect cooperation...."

"The parsonage kitchen *is* inadequate. Only two burners on the stove work, and there is no cupboard or counter space. If you could help us get it remodeled that would be wonderful. You'd be a hero to my wife. But our kitchen has nothing to do with Miss Emily's safe; we'll open it when Mr. Yost returns."

The lawyer turned pink and then red as he stared at Calvin Chamberlain. Without another word Mr. Wilson carefully placed his coffee cup in the saucer and strode out to his car.

"I know nothing about legal matters," Calvin admitted, "but I'm here if you need me." He left a few minutes later.

After lunch Emily set out on foot to investigate a *pop-pop* motor sound she had been hearing all day. It came from the other side of the beaver pond. Rather than risk meeting Keith Cavanaugh, she walked down the lane and turned right to walk along the road. Beyond the pond, she saw the source of the noise. A bulldozer was cutting an ugly gash through the woods. Trees fell in the path of the huge machine.

Signs had been nailed to the trees beside the road. Berkshire Vista. Building Sites. Custom Built Vacation Homes. Private Swimming and Boating. Elegance. Culture. Prestige. Pittsfield Development Corp.

Emily picked up a stick and hit it against a tree. She looked up to see Jay LaRoux grinning at her from his car. He saluted and drove off. She marched back to the Gilberts to announce the desecration of their hills.

"Can't think there's anything we can do." Ruth was in the kitchen preparing beans for the freezer, and she spoke without slowing her hands. "They own the land. Wonder where they're going to dig a lake for that swimming and boating you say they're advertising?"

Emily sat down at the big kitchen table, picked up a knife, and began to cut the ends off the beans while

Ruth blanched them and put them in plastic bags. They worked in silence for a long time.

"I don't suppose it will matter," Emily said. "They'll be on the other side of the beaver pond—unless Mr. Wilson is right and they own the beaver pond. You don't suppose they could turn it into a lake for swimming and boating right in my front yard?"

"You own the beaver pond," Ruth reassured her.

When the beans were all ready for the freezer, Emily went home to find Nika sitting under a tree with a sketch pad.

"Had this yen to sketch," she explained briefly and went on with her work while Emily called the dogs to dinner. They had obviously been visiting Keith, which explained how Nika had been allowed to get out of her car.

Nika tore a rough sketch of the house off her pad and handed it to Emily. "Now you sit over there and let's see what I can do."

Emily sat on the bottom step of her verandah. Job joined her.

"If it isn't beauty and the beast," laughed Nika. "That's the ugliest dog I ever saw."

"I beg your pardon, and yours too, Job. This dog may not be a creature of great physical charm, but he has a beautiful soul. Don't you, love?"

Job licked her face affectionately, as if he knew she was defending his character. Nika sketched on until the light began to fade and Emily was getting bored. Then she accepted Emily's invitation to dinner and listened to her tirade against the Pittsfield Development Corporation.

"Enough," Nika said at last. "You may not like to see the woods cut down for summer houses, but think what it will do for the town. It will increase the tax base for one thing. For another, people who can afford summer houses can also afford art. Think of all those beautiful bare walls in all those brand new houses.

Makes my mouth water in anticipation. I'll stock more large pieces next year."

Nika stood up from the table, shook out her tent of a dress, and waddled off to her car.

Emily stood in the doorway. "Thanks," she called after her guest.

"What for?" Nika's voice came out of the darkness.

"For hiring me this summer and…"

Nika drove off into the night.

…for listening…for being a friend.

The next day Emily received a phone call from a man who said he worked with Mrs. Cook. He and his wife would like to rent the octagonal room for Friday and Saturday nights. Mrs. Cook had told him that the price would be fifty dollars a night, including breakfast. On Thursday Nika sent a woman and her young daughter to her. So once again she had a full house for the weekend.

The following Tuesday morning Emily had unexpected guests. The dogs began barking while Emily was finishing her breakfast. As she ran out the back door, she heard Keith ordering the dogs to sit. Coming around the house she saw that they had obeyed and were sitting side-by-side in the driveway watching Keith and another man escorting a bent woman. The woman, who appeared to be in her late twenties, walked as if each step she took was agony. Her pale face, beneath a cap of dark hair, was etched with pain.

"Bring her in the front way," Emily shouted and ran back through the house to unbolt the big door. She stepped out on the verandah as the men stood helplessly by while the woman slowly hoisted her slender body up the few steps, holding tightly to the railing.

"Nathan and Betz Benson," said Keith briefly. "Emily Stanoszek."

"It's a muscle spasm," Nathan explained. "Comes on without warning. We'd just arrived at Keith's camp and

145

whammo. She needs a firm bed and medication."

"She's welcome to my bed, but the best bed is upstairs in the front room. Could she make it up those stairs?"

The woman nodded and crept across the hallway and started up the stairs, clinging to the banister.

"Shouldn't we carry her?" asked Keith.

"She manages better by herself." Nathan took a bottle out of his wife's purse and shook out two pills.

Emily got a glass of water and rushed past the woman to turn back the bed, glad that she had prepared the room as soon as her last guests left. She opened the bathroom door so its location would be obvious and then went back to the verandah while Nathan put his wife to bed. Keith was sitting on the swing.

"Sorry to bother you like this," he said without looking at her.

"What's the bother? This is a bed-and-breakfast establishment. I don't serve lunch or dinner but I could make an exception for your friends."

"You'll be paid your usual rates."

How could that man sit there on her verandah and talk to her as if she were a stranger? She was furious with him. Fortunately, Nathan appeared before she had a chance to explode. He asked if they could spend the night and perhaps the next; he also wanted to use her phone to cancel their reservations.

"It's in the kitchen." Keith started to lead the way.

"Wait. I'll go first," said Emily. "You'll upset my guard dog."

"Job is outside," Keith said without stopping.

"I'm referring to my little guard dog."

All four pups were still in their night box. Just as Emily knew he would be, Billy was standing with his paws on the edge of the box trying to scramble out. He was yipping furiously. There was even a hint of a growl. She lifted him to the floor where he trotted right up to Keith, slipping only twice. He planted his tiny front paws and began to yip again.

"Hey, he is ferocious," laughed Nathan. "Five pounds of tiger. Betz will love him."

While Nathan dialed, Emily picked up Billy and took him to his daytime box outside. "You really told them a thing or two," she giggled.

When she went back to bring the others out she explained that Kappy was going to be adopted by Buddy. Keith nodded his approval and picked up Hugh and Kezia. "I'm hoping Josie Peck will take Hugh. They were instantly attracted to one another."

"What about Kezia?" he asked.

"I still have to find homes for Kezia and Billy."

"You won't give up Billy."

How did he know what she might or might not do?

When Nathan was off the phone, he and Emily made arrangements for Betz. Keith turned his back and walked out on the back porch. Nathan would stay with his wife while Emily went into town to buy a heating pad and food. When she came back, Nathan would go out to the pond and spend the day with Keith. Betz would probably sleep most of the day and feel better when she awoke. They'd all have dinner in the bedroom upstairs.

The day went as planned. By late afternoon Betz was awake. She was still in pain but she took a shower, put on a nightie and robe, and climbed back into bed propped up on pillows. Emily brought iced tea upstairs and the two women enjoyed a get-acquainted chat.

Betz talked about her two children who were visiting their grandparents at a lake in Minnesota. Emily told about inheriting the house and about her guests.

"And Keith?" asked Betz. "How is he making out? He's one of my favorite people, but I worry about him."

"He seems remarkably self-sufficient." Emily told

147

how he had delivered the pups and about the explosion at the dam the next night. "I haven't seen him since then," she added.

"But you were together when the dam exploded?"

"He'd taken me to dinner." Emily turned away from Betz's inquisitive eyes. "I don't know if he'll come to dinner tonight or not. Probably not."

"He'll be here," Betz said confidently. "Nathan is his best friend."

Emily set up the card table and chairs and excused herself to fix dinner.

Keith did come to dinner and went immediately upstairs to see his friends. Emily greeted him as she placed the silver on the card table.

"When you're ready to bring the food up, call me," Keith said. He had been in her house for half an hour and that was the first sentence he had directed to her.

Emily boiled the corn and then put it on a tray with a platter of fried chicken and a plate of sliced tomatoes. Then she did call Keith who carried it upstairs while Emily tagged along behind with the potato salad.

"Terrific," Nathan announced as the food was set out. "You're a lucky man, Keith, to have a neighbor who is one of the prettiest women I've ever seen and who can cook too. Is your hand spoken for?" he asked, bowing before her.

Emily blushed. Keith scowled. Betz caught her husband's eye with a warning look to "hush."

Keith ate in stony silence, but Nathan regaled them with funny stories. When they had finished everything in sight, Nathan loaded the dirty dishes on the tray and carried it downstairs. He stood watching Emily as she scooped out sherbet and loaded it on the tray with the coffee mugs.

"You may be having some difficulty understanding Keith," he said. "Ask Betz to explain him to you tomorrow. We're both very fond of him. He's really one great guy and the work he's doing is important."

Not knowing what to say, Emily said nothing.

Betz began to wince in pain during the dessert. She tried to cover it, but it was obvious that she wanted nothing so much as to take more pain pills and sleep. Emily gulped down the rest of her coffee, filled Nathan's mug again, and loaded everything else on the tray. Keith picked it up. At the door, he turned.

"Hope you feel better in the morning, Betz."

Betz answered with a small wave of her hand.

"I'll read your manuscript tonight so we can discuss it in the morning," Nathan said to Keith. "Thanks, Emily, for everything. If this had to happen, it couldn't have happened at a better place."

"My pleasure," Emily said and meant it. "Breakfast will be set up in my sitting room whenever you want it. I'll leave the tray there so you can take it upstairs. Good night."

Keith put the tray down by the kitchen sink and stood watching Emily as she busied herself putting away food and washing the dishes. Then he picked up a towel and began to dry. He said not a word. The silence was awkward.

"Your friends are pleasant people," Emily volunteered.

"The best."

"Betz is obviously in a lot of pain. I wonder if she has these attacks often."

"A couple of times a year, Nathan says. They only last a day or two. They'd like to stay tomorrow if they may. They'll be leaving on Thursday." Keith took the sponge from her hand and wiped fingerprints off the refrigerator door.

"You're good kitchen help."

"Years of experience." He put the sponge down. "Time to bring in the pups?"

She nodded.

He went out to the back porch. "Where's your

mighty watchdog?" he called.

"What do you mean?" She ran out and peered into the box where three puppies were busy batting at one another and rolling in the paper. Before she had moved the big box outside, she had carefully barricaded the low section where Billy had previously escaped. The barricade was still in place. "Billy," she called urgently. "Where are you, Billy?"

Beyond the rays of the porch light it was dark. Job barked once. Emily ran for her flashlight and went out to where Keith was standing on the lawn looking down. She shone the light on a puppy whose father was nudging him in the direction of the house. The pup had set his front feet and was yipping up at Keith who was chuckling down at him.

Emily picked up Billy with one hand and reached down to pat Job with the other. "What a good father you are," she cooed.

"I hate to tell you this, Job," said Keith, "but I'm afraid your younger son has a wayward streak in him. He'll be stealing cars before you know it."

"He will not," Emily glared at Keith. "He's a good puppy. He just has more courage than the others, probably because getting born was such an ordeal for him." She put the puppy against her neck and carried him to the house. Keith followed with Kappy and Hugh and went back for Kezia.

"Everybody has a home but you," he said as he stroked her. "Poor Kezia. You're such a pretty puppy and have the nicest name in the lot."

"Would you like to adopt Kezia?" Emily asked hopefully.

"No, I've learned my lesson. I'll never have anything to do with attractive females of any breed." He put Kezia in the box and turned to the door, letting it slam behind him.

Emily ran after him. "Good night, Keith," she called.

150

To her surprise, he came back on the porch. "I've been rude to you."

"Yes, you have."

"And you've been so kind to me and my friends. You're just too good to be true...so beautiful, so...beautiful." He placed his hands on her shoulders, drew her to him slowly, and kissed her. After a few moments he pushed her away. "Sorry. I shouldn't have done that."

"Did you hear me complaining?" Emily laughed softly.

He scowled. "This is all wrong." He sprinted across the lawn.

Nathan spent most of the following day at the beaver pond. And, over a shared lunch on the verandah, Betz helped Emily understand a little more about Keith.

He had been married for three years to a lovely, feminine girl who had been a student in a class he taught while he was getting his doctorate. "I don't think I ever heard her say anything original in the three years I knew her, but she had a beautiful smile and men were smitten by her. You can bet your last dollar that I stayed close to Nathan's side whenever she was around." Betz laughed. "She enjoyed being waited on—and Keith waited on her. She never invited us to dinner, though we lived near one another and I was forever feeding them. She didn't even help with the dishes. No one seemed to expect the poor darling to do anything.

"Then a famous author visited the campus for a semester. He had just written his first best seller, complete with big contracts with a paperback house and a movie company. When the semester was over he packed up his car with his books, his clothes, and Keith's wife. She hadn't even bothered to tell Keith she was going.

"She hated scenes," explained Betz. "We were with him when he received her note saying she was sorry but the other man was making a lot of money and would take her to Paris and Rome. Besides, he didn't want her to have a baby."

"That's cruel," Emily whispered.

"Especially the line about the baby. We'd had Nate by then and Keith was crazy about him. Keith is Nate's godfather. I guess he thought his wife should have a baby too. We heard that she married the author on the day the divorce was final. Afterward, Keith came east to Williams. I hadn't seen him again until yesterday, but he and Nathan often talk on the phone, and every Christmas—and sometimes on no special day at all— he sends the most wonderful books to Nate and Liz. He's never even seen Liz. He left five years ago and so far as I know he's never looked at another woman since."

The two women sat looking out toward the beaver pond, neither of them seeing it.

"It's none of my business, Emily," Betz said softly. "but you're very beautiful. Keith certainly doesn't act like your lover but you do seem to upset him. I don't know if you find him attractive or not. If not, please don't toy with him. He's too vulnerable. But, if you do want him, you'll have to go after him. Personally, I think you'd make a terrific pair."

"I'm passive too, like his wife," said Emily flatly.

Betz stared at her, open-mouthed. "I don't believe that. You came to this town knowing no one. You put this house in order and are renting rooms to make it pay. You told me you like your work in the gallery. You're not passive. Maybe you've just never wanted anything enough to take a stand until this house fell into your lap…"

"Thank you for telling me about Keith," Emily said. "Now I have to see about dinner."

She served dinner in her sitting room. It was a jolly

152

affair during which the men talked on and on about Keith's book. Keith left before his friends went upstairs.

The next day Betz was walking uprightly and the Bensons drove on to Woods Hole. They had left an envelope in their room with a grateful note and a check for one hundred dollars.

That afternoon Keith walked over to her house. "Wanted to pay for the food my friends ate," he said curtly.

"No charge," said Emily, just as curtly. "They paid a fair price for their room. That's enough."

"But you bought a lot of food and worked hard preparing meals for them. I insist on paying."

"I refuse." Emily's chin lifted in a most assertive way.

He shrugged his shoulders and walked back to his camp.

She stood watching him, aware of the *put-putting* of the bulldozer still ravaging the woods. There was a roll of thunder in the distance. That night it poured. Emily sat on her verandah and watched the lightning and thought about all Betz had said.

Chapter Eleven

Friday morning was bright and clear. Emily jumped out of bed, determined to clean her own quarters thoroughly before she went to work at the gallery. Suddenly she heard a *put-put* and a roaring of gears—disturbingly near.

She pulled on her jeans, stuffing her pajama top in at the waist, and shoved her feet into sneakers. She ran toward the noise with Job and Bertha at her heels. The lane ended at a huge tree and a strip of woods. Beyond was the corn field. She ran through the woods and stopped, staring, as a bulldozer plowed its way through the bottom section of the field, crushing the corn under its treads.

"That's my land!" she shouted as she ran directly into the face of the dozer, shaking her fist at the driver.

She was vaguely aware of running footsteps on both sides of her as the dozer quieted to a steady *put-put*. The driver motioned her out of his way.

"I will not move!" she shouted.

Bertha ran off toward the beaver pond but Job stood staunchly in front of her. The driver jumped out of the cab and approached her. So did Keith from one side and Gil Gilbert from the other.

"Look, lady," the driver said, "I don't know who you are but I have my orders, and my orders are to make a road through this corn patch and those woods to connect with the lane over there. That's what I intend to do, so get out of my way." He went back to his cab without waiting for an answer.

"You will not move one inch," Emily shouted at him. She pushed corn stalks aside and sat down in front of the dozer, holding Job in her arms.

The driver gunned his motor.

"Run over me—if you want to be tried for murder."

"You tell him, Em." Keith laughed from the sidelines.

"This is not funny." Emily glared at him.

He sobered immediately. "No, it's not. May I use your phone to call the troopers?"

"Call John Chamberlain too," she said.

The driver climbed out of his cab again. "I'm gonna call the boss," he said, following Keith.

Gil came toward her with a crushed cob. "I hadn't harvested that section."

Ruth and Tommy Gilbert came through the field and stood by Gil, looking down at Emily and Job still sitting in front of the dozer. Then all three Gilberts began to rip ears of corn from the stalks in the path of the huge destroyer. They worked frantically, tossing the ears behind them. Emily got up and helped, at the same time trying to assure the Gilberts that it wasn't necessary.

"This is my land and I will not let that road go through. I'm sorry about the damage that's already been done. It will not go any further."

Even as she was speaking, her alter ego was whispering encouragement. *Is this Emily Stanoszek, the woman with the backbone of a butterfly? The woman who two days ago accused herself of being passive? My, my, how you've changed!*

She saw Keith and the dozer driver approaching and ran back to her post in front of the machine. She staggered, almost falling. She felt so lightheaded. She had

156

not had anything to eat and the hot sun was burning her fair skin. She refused to faint. Fainting was for ladies like Grace, not Emily. Keith ran toward her and put his arm around her and began to murmur soothing words.

"Stop cooing," she ordered, pushing him away. "I can take care of this."

The state police car drove into the lane, followed by another car with a man in a business suit and Wilbert Wilson.

"What seems to be the problem?" asked the trooper.

"This dozer is ripping up my land and the corn field I'm renting to the Gilberts," Emily stated flatly. "Please tell him to back up and keep his land destroyer off my property."

"This is my property, bought and paid for in full." The man in the business suit pulled a sheaf of papers from his attaché case, waving them in front of the trooper. "You may have noticed our signs. We are developing this area. That ugly ghost of a pond will be dredged for swimming and boating. There will be attractive vacation houses all around it—"

"Oh no, you don't!" Keith stepped forward, his arms folded across his chest. "Beavers live in that pond. They've been there for generations, and they'll continue to live there. I've told Miss Stanoszek that if she wishes to sell the beaver pond, I'll buy it."

The trooper looked at the papers. Emily noticed Calvin Chamberlain emerge from the woods and stand quietly at the back of the little crowd.

"I'm sorry for this unpleasantness." It was Wilbert Wilson's turn. "I've tried to explain to Miss Stanoszek that Peter Darrow sold this land to the Pittsfield Development Corporation, everything up to the lane and in a straight line from the end of the lane through to the edge of the property. You'll see that the bill of sale is in order. I drew it up myself."

Emily looked over the trooper's shoulder. "I don't

157

think that is Peter Darrow's signature," she said pointing to a line at the bottom of the first sheet. "Besides, that paper is dated August of last year. If he sold it, why did he pay school taxes on it in September and town taxes in February? Mr. Yost has his canceled checks."

She turned to the man in the business suit. "Did you pay taxes on this land?"

"I never got a bill," he said.

"So Peter Darrow paid the taxes," laughed Wilson. "Some mix-up with the collector. Or Darrow's senility. He was eighty-seven years old."

"Peter Darrow was old; he was not senile." Keith spoke firmly.

The trooper looked from one person to another, shaking his head in bewilderment.

"Maybe you'd like to see the stakes?" Ruth suggested tentatively.

"Yeah. That's a good idea." The trooper seemed relieved to be doing something, anything, rather than listening to all these angry people.

They all marched around the bulldozer and walked in its path over crushed corn stalks. The Gilberts looked devastated and Emily put her arm around Ruth They walked south along the edge of the cornfield to the corner. Gil ran ahead.

"There it—" He stopped and began pushing the corn aside, then the brush that grew outside the cornfield. "It was here when I planted the field."

"You probably knocked it down with your tractor," the trooper said.

"I did not."

Without a word they turned back and walked across the dozer tracks through the woods intersected by beaver canals, but no stake was there either.

"You can't accuse me of knocking that one down," Gil said.

"Who owns the land on the other side?" Emily asked.

"We do," answered the man from the development corporation.

"All of it? Behind the Gilbert farm too?"

"Just a little beyond where we're building this road. Jay LaRoux owns the rest. He's offered to sell but his price is ridiculous. We might...nevermind what we might do." He turned to the dozer driver. "We've wasted enough time. Get on with your work."

"You will not go forward," Emily said. "I'll sit in front of that dozer all day if necessary. Of course, he can always run over me."

Everyone turned to the helpless trooper again. He shuffled his feet and scratched his ear.

John Chamberlain stepped forward. "I'm one of the two executors of Mr. Darrow's estate," he said, introducing himself to the trooper. "The other executor—and by far the more experienced one—is James Yost who is out of town. He'll be back Monday at the latest. We think that the deed to the property is in a safe in the house. When Mr. Yost returns, we'll open the safe. If the deed is there, it should settle this question of ownership. Couldn't we just wait until Mr. Yost returns?"

The trooper grinned. "Right. You just back up the dozer and Tuesday you can talk to Yost." The trooper addressed the businessman.

At last he agreed and they all stood silently while the dozer driver backed his machine along the path he had made. The Gilberts sent Tommy back to the house for bushel baskets and continued their harvest. Everyone else drove off, with Job running along behind them barking.

Emily started toward the house with Keith at her side.

"Spirited wench," he said softly.

She turned away from him and went inside, leaving him to stare after her from the lane.

An hour later she was at the gallery, feeling a mixture

159

of pride—she really had stood up for her rights—and doubt—did she own the land or not? She also felt exhausted.

Saturday Emily awoke at dawn, thoroughly chilled by an early fall cold front. She found herself another blanket and went back to bed. Poor Nika had hoped for a bang-up Labor Day weekend to provide a smashing conclusion to a profitable summer. When Emily awoke again a few hours later, her house was still cold and she put on jeans and a periwinkle-blue sweat shirt. The puppies lay huddled together in their box. Emily built a fire in her stove to take the chill off the room.

When she left for the gallery at noon, the sky was still heavy with dark, moist clouds. She greeted the Gilberts in the almost empty flea market. They had plenty of vegetables but few customers. Those few who came into the gallery were lookers more intent on finding shelter from the cold wind than in buying beautiful things. Emily and Nika drank mugs of coffee and discussed the season ahead. Nika would be open weekends only until Color Weekend, in the middle of October. Then she would close the gallery and head for Florida to take advantage of the tourist season there.

"Want to come with me?" Nika asked. "I've been thinking of opening a branch gallery in Orlando. You could run it."

Emily shook her head. "I can't make any plans until the estate is settled and the pups have found homes," she said. "But thanks. I suspect that by the first of January I'll be sorry I turned you down. Josie tells me that winters here are grim, and I don't suppose there's a job to be found. It'll be lonely."

The door banged open and Eddy strode into the gallery. "Just had a call from the professor. Emergency. He told me to bring you home immediately."

She followed him to her car, handed him the keys,

and they drove off with a squeal of tires.

"What is it?" she asked anxiously.

"I don't know. He didn't say, and he hung up before I could ask him."

Fire? She hadn't heard a siren. The bulldozer again? Why hadn't Keith called her directly? There was a phone in the gallery.

They drove into the driveway beside a state trooper's car, but no one came to greet her. Where were Job and Bertha? Why didn't they bark? And then she saw Keith and the trooper staring down at something on the edge of the woods. Another car drove up and a man Emily recognized as the vet got out with his bag and ran toward the woods.

Emily followed reluctantly, Eddy at her side, until she could see both dogs lying on the ground. Job had dragged himself some distance, leaving a trail of blood on the grass. She looked at Bertha who was lying perfectly still, as if asleep. When she knelt down by Job, he tried to raise his head but he could not. She reached out to stroke him.

"Careful," said the vet. "He's hurt, and hurt dogs are unpredictable. Let me have a look at you, old boy." He turned the dog over revealing a stomach oozing blood. He prodded with gentle fingers. "The bullet is there," he said to the trooper. Then he turned to Emily. "Is this your dog?" he asked.

She nodded, biting her lip. Eddy stroked her back.

"There's nothing to be done for him," he said gently, "Except to end his pain. May I have your permission to put him to sleep?"

"There's nothing else you can do for him?" Emily asked in a pleading voice. "He has a very strong constitution."

"The bullet is too close to his heart. His lungs are badly damaged. Several of his ribs are shattered."

She gulped and nodded. While the vet prepared the hypodermic needle, she sat beside Job and stroked his head. "You've been a good, faithful friend," she whispered. "I couldn't have lived here this summer without you." The dog licked her hand weakly. "If heaven is open to dogs, you and Bertha will go there together. Peter will be glad to see you. If I have to leave here, tell him that I did my best." She wiped at tears that were streaming out of her eyes.

All four of the men had been standing back while she said good-by to Job. The vet stepped forward and inserted the needle. It was over.

"Stand aside now," he said gently. "I'm going to remove the bullet. The police may want it for evidence."

Emily walked slowly over to Bertha. She saw blood on the grass under the big dog's head. Otherwise, she looked perfectly peaceful. "Good-by, Bertha," she whispered. "You'll have Job to take care of you so don't be afraid. I'll see that your pups all have good homes. You can be sure of that."

Eddy lifted her to her feet. Keith came out of her garage with a shovel. "Here?" he asked, indicating a spot at the edge of the woods.

Emily nodded. "In one grave."

She leaned against the garage while Keith and Eddy took turns digging the deep hole. The vet worked on Job for a few more minutes and then handed the bullet to the trooper who put it in a plastic bag. Then he removed the bullet from Bertha and gave it to the trooper too. The vet drove off without another word.

The trooper came and stood looking down at her. "Have you any idea who did this?"

She shook her head.

"They were both shot at close range. Dr. Cavanaugh said he heard the shots. He ran over, saw what had happened, and then ran to the Gilberts to phone. The times seem to line up. I have to ask you this question: do you think the professor could have shot your dogs?"

"No. I know that Keith Cavanaugh could not have

162

killed these dogs or any other animal. I know that for sure. I don't know anything else."

"I'm sorry," he said. "You've had a lot of trouble out here. Dr. Cavanaugh suggested that someone has been trying to scare you away and that the dogs might have been killed to make you easier to frighten."

"I can't stay here without them."

The radio in the trooper's car crackled, and he got in and drove off. Still Keith and Eddy continued to dig. At last they lowered Bertha into the hole and then Job. Emily, remembering Peter's burial, stepped forward and dropped a handful of dirt onto their bodies. "The Lord give you peace," she said and walked to her house and sat on the back porch steps. From inside, she could hear the puppies yipping. It had been too cold to put them outside, so she had covered the floor of the pantry with newspapers and barricaded the doorway into the kitchen before she left for work. She went inside and picked up Billy, whom she wrapped in a towel for warmth, and brought him out to sit on the steps with her. There was comfort in his warm, wiggling body.

Keith put the shovel back in the garage. "I'm sorry," he said softly and then walked quickly down her driveway toward his camp.

Eddy came and sat beside her, saying nothing. Emily, numb in her grief, nevertheless remembered the last time she had seen Eddy, the time she had vowed never to ask anything of him again.

"Thank you, Eddy," she whispered. "Please go now. There is nothing more to be done."

Eddy patted her shoulder. "You need me now, more than ever. You'll be afraid."

"I'll be leaving as soon as I find homes for the pups. Please go."

At last he got up, walked slowly to the woods, and then jogged off down the trail toward town.

When he was out of sight, Emily went and stood beside the fresh grave, holding Billy close. She shivered, partly from cold and partly from shock. The utterly senseless violence! She thought of other deaths in her life. Her parents had died violently, but she had no memory of that. Both her grandparents had died peacefully, from natural causes. She had grieved for them, but it was a grief tinged with regret for things she had not said or done, situations and tensions she had not understood.

Bertha and Job were only dogs, and she had known them for just four months. They had given wholeheartedly and asked nothing in return. They had trusted her. Her love for them was not shrouded in regret or guilt. She stood there, beside their grave, and sobbed uncontrollably while little Billy slept in her arms.

She looked down at him. Of all the puppies, he was the one most like his father both in appearance and spirit. If she could give him up now, she would save herself from a repetition of the grief she was feeling. But she could not part with this pup, Job's son.

At last the tears dried up, leaving only a barren ache. She walked slowly back to the house and called Nika to tell her she would not be back at the gallery until the following day.

She fed the pups and made herself a cup of tea and a piece of toast. Both grew cold on the table as Emily sat huddled in Job's chair. It grew dark outside. The days were short now. The room grew chilly. Still Emily sat.

She was roused by the sound of a knock on the door. She had a sudden vision of Keith and ran to open it eagerly. It was Nika. She had driven up, parked her car in the driveway, and there had been no warning bark. Loneliness flooded Emily's soul. Nika had come because she was kind. The trouble was that Nika could not share her grief. Keith could have done that.

"Sorry about all this," Nika said as she stepped into the kitchen. She took one look at the full cup of cold tea and the limp toast and busied herself making more tea and toast and building a fire.

"Sit down and eat," she ordered.

Emily obeyed. Nika talked endlessly; she talked about the success of the gallery this year, about her plans for next year in Florida and in Stonefield, about crazy customers, about the wonderful things Emily had done with the house. Emily hardly heard her. At last Nika seemed to wind down.

"Good grief, Emily," she said at last. "They were dogs, not people. You have four other dogs, after all. So snap out of it."

Emily stared at her incredulously. "Thank you for trying to help," she said. She stood up, willing Nika to leave.

"You'll feel better tomorrow, old dear." Nika planted a kiss on Emily's cheek and left.

Why hadn't Keith come instead of Nika? Why had he sent Eddy to get her at the gallery and then why had he left Eddy to comfort her once the dogs were buried? Because he didn't care about her. That was the only answer. Maybe he had cared briefly on the evening after the pups were delivered. He'd ignored her since then. Never had she felt so abandoned. She locked her house carefully and went to bed.

The next morning, Emily approached the fresh grave and stopped in surprise. Someone had planted a miniature rose bush at the head of the grave. The tiny yellow buds were exquisite. Had Keith planted it? She hoped so.

The day was just as cold and drear as the preceding one had been, but there were a few more customers in the gallery during the early afternoon. Emily began the day waiting on a woman who insisted on telling her, in strident tones, how art used to be when a flower looked like a flower, when it required talent to be an artist. Emily was too listless to argue, and she directed the woman to the small framed floral prints. She bought six of them, Emily's only sale that day.

At six o'clock Nika said that business was too poor to bother keeping the gallery open any longer. She drew the shade on the door and flipped the sign that read "Closed." They counted the cash and Nika offered to drive her home. Emily insisted on walking and then wished she had not. It was a mournful trudge along her lane and into the darkening drive with no welcoming barks. She stopped again at the grave and picked a perfect rose bud, which she took into the house and put in a small vase.

She walked through the pantry to her sitting room and was about to switch on the TV when a muffled thud from somewhere upstairs started her pulse racing. Her first thought was of Job. How could she face an emergency without him?

A weapon? She ran to the pantry and picked up a hammer and then slowly opened the door to the hall and crept out. The front door was ajar. Surely she had locked it. She closed it quietly and started up the steps, stopping on each one to listen, hearing nothing. Maybe it had all been her imagination. She was on edge; her ears were playing tricks on her. Almost convinced, she crossed the landing and ascended the second flight.

Through the open door of the back bedroom, she could see that it was just as she had left it, ready for guests who would probably not come this late in the season. She gasped aloud when she reached the doorway of the octagonal bedroom. The wood paneling above the mantle had been ripped out, exposing the brick of the chimney behind it. She had a brief glimpse of well-padded buttocks before Wilbert Wilson withdrew his head from the fireplace and turned around.

"What are you doing here?" Emily's voice quavered. His smile did not reassure her. As he came toward

166

her, she edged into the room and stood with her hands behind her grasping the hammer, leaning against the wall for support. He followed her eyes to the splintered paneling.

"Sorry about that," he said nonchalantly. "But I really must have that deed, and you have been so unreasonable, my dear. Now if you'll just tell me where it is, you can see that I have brought tools to open the safe." He indicated a drill that was already plugged into an outlet. "It must be somewhere near the fireplace. Just tell your Uncle Will where it is." He came closer and Emily cringed. "Don't be afraid of me, my dear. I am your lawyer. I have your best interests at heart. It really hurts me to have to frighten you a little."

"*You* threw the rock in my window and punctured the water pipe?"

"No harm done," he said soothingly. "Now where is the safe?"

"Bertha and Job? Did you kill them too?"

"They were vicious dogs. I disposed of them for your own protection, my dear, and for the good of the community. Now if you'll just tell me the location of the safe..."

"No. I will not."

He switched on the overhead light, and she could see that his eyes were blazing. Then he grabbed her and raised her up on her toes. "Tell me where that safe is. Now."

"No," she whispered, terrified by the look in his eyes.

Still holding her in one hand, he slapped her across the face with the other so that tears came to her eyes. "Tell me," he demanded, raising his hand to slap her again.

Without thinking she swung her hammer into his stomach. He screamed in pain and began to swear, but he held on to her sweater and shirt. She pulled away and ran—across the hall, down the stairs, across the downstairs hall, and out the front door.

It was totally dark. She twisted her ankle on a rock and fell, but picked herself up and ran on, limping. Across the lane, she began to scream.

"Help me! Please Keith, help me!" She searched in the dark for the pathway to his camp, then gave up and took off through the brush, feeling the sting of the branches against her body. She fell again, painfully. Gasping for breath, she struggled to her knees. Suddenly she was engulfed in light. The light went out and she was lifted into strong arms, her head nestled against a silky beard.

"Emily, what's wrong? Are you hurt? Tell me, Em!" His voice was hoarse.

"Oh, Keith—in the house—he tried to make me tell him where the safe is!"

"Are you all right? Did he hurt you—"

"No, no, I'm okay—"

"Oh my darling Em," Keith whispered as he turned with her in his arms. Together they strode back to the lane and then ran toward the house.

He ran up onto the verandah and went cautiously through the open front door. He stood a moment, staring, in amazement as Emily, anxious for the touch of him, came beside him and ducked under his arm. He held her tightly as they watched Wilbert Wilson crawling painfully backward down the stairs.

"Stay right there," Keith ordered.

"She tried to kill me." The lawyer held his stomach and sank to a sitting position on the bottom step. His face was gray. The long strands of hair that usually covered his balding head had fallen from the part to cover his ear. "She hit me with a hammer," he hissed.

"Good," said Keith, matter-of-factly.

Then he turned to look at Emily in the light. "You're a mass of scratches but none of them seem deep. Your left ankle is swelling. Come on Tiger." He phoned the troopers then led her to the bathroom where he turned on the water to fill the tub.

She soaked in the comforting water and washed her hair. Feeling too tired to dry it, she wrapped her head in a towel and put on a pair of soft blue sweat pants and shirt. Her body was sore and her ankle hurt.

She could smell fresh coffee as she went through the kitchen and saw that Keith had set up the pot in her sitting room. Through the open door she could see Wilbert Wilson being supported by a trooper as he left through the front door.

"He says you hit him with a hammer," said another trooper, the same one who had come when she tried to stop the bulldozer.

"I did," said Emily.

"Good girl," whispered Keith as he pushed her down on the cot and put a mug of coffee in her hand.

"He threw a rock through my window. He punched holes in the pipe in my spring house. Yesterday he shot Bertha and Job." A sob rose in her throat.

"The dogs," Keith explained to the startled trooper.

Questioned carefully, she described what had happened that night. Keith held her hand.

"Is there a safe?" the trooper asked when she had finished. "And is the deed in the safe?"

"There is definitely a safe. I don't know what's in it."

"I'd like to see it," the trooper said. "It must be well hidden. Wilson certainly tore the room apart trying to find it. Is it in that room? Wilson brought a drill along, but I won't try to open it. I'm just curious."

"Turn the hook on the left-hand wall of the closet. You'll see it."

The trooper and Keith went upstairs and returned in a few minutes.

"Clever man, that Peter Darrow," said Keith.

"Very clever." The trooper sat down and stared at the floor. "I don't really know what the charges are," he said. "There's vandalism."

169

"And murder. He murdered two wonderful dogs."

"There must be a law against killing pets, but I don't know the penalty. I'll look into it."

"Don't forget assault, not to mention breaking and entering," said Keith angrily.

"He had a key. He said Miss Emily gave it to him."

"I did not. He must have had it made before he gave me Peter Darrow's keys. And that's why he killed the dogs. So he'd have free access to the house. I usually work late at the gallery. He must have thought he could open the safe and get away before I returned."

"You look worn out," the trooper said to Emily. "We'll need a signed statement from you later, but I'm going now. We'll get in touch with Yost as soon as possible and open the safe. There may be a clue there. Then we'll decide what to do next. I don't think you need to worry about Wilson prosecuting you."

"Prosecuting *me?*" Emily's eyes were wide with incredulity. "I didn't do anything except protect myself!"

"You hit him with a deadly weapon." The trooper laughed and went out.

Keith walked to the door with him. When he came back he took the towel off Emily's head and began to dry her hair. "Who would have believed you could ...you're so pretty, Em," he sighed, kissing her nose. "I adore you."

His hands were strong and tender and she began to relax.

"Go to bed, Em." he said at last, pulling her to her feet. "I'll clean up here."

When she was in bed, he came and sat beside her and stroked her hand and told her how brave she had been and how pretty she was and...she fell asleep.

She awoke with Keith's finger stroking her cheek and opened her eyes to see him smiling at her. He kissed her forehead and handed her a mug of coffee.

"Mr. Yost returned last night and knows all about

170

what happened here. You may have forgotten that this is Labor Day. Nevertheless, he and the trooper who was here last night and a locksmith are on their way. I told Mr. Yost that I had just dropped by to see how you were and that you were out with the pups. Didn't want to compromise your reputation by letting him think I was here all night."

"Were you?"

"Yes. I slept on your cot. It sags. I thought you might have nightmares or something, but you slept like a baby. Now get dressed on the double." He turned and walked out of her room.

Her muscles were stiff; but she did as bidden, dressing quickly in tan slacks and shirt and a green sweater. She put on socks and loafers. If she was supposed to have been out early with the pups, she would surely be wearing shoes.

She was waiting at the front door to greet the two executors of the estate, the locksmith, and the trooper when they arrived. Keith had disappeared. Without so much as a "good morning," Yost stood directly in front of her and said, "I owe you an apology. I should not have gone away before this was settled. I did not trust Wilson. I never have. You must believe, however, that I had no idea he would resort to violence. I am most truly sorry."

"How could you have known? I thought he was a fatherly old darling." She smiled at the banker and thought how she had misjudged him. The banker was the darling—cold and pale, but courtly and kind.

They walked upstairs together and Mr. Yost actually smiled when she turned the clothes hook and the wall swung open.

"I should tell you that I found a journal sitting on top of the safe. I have read it and will give it to you if you think necessary, though I would rather not. Mr. Darrow met my grandmother, Grace Gresham, when she came to visit her uncle, the local parson. He

171

thought she was going to marry him and built this house for her. Instead she married my grandfather and Peter went to Alaska. The journal is about the house and about his love for her. It's very personal."

"Then we don't need to read it," said Calvin Chamberlain.

Emily suspected that the trooper was disappointed but he said nothing.

They all stepped back to give the locksmith room. He tried one blank key and then another until he found one that seemed to please him. He took it out of the lock and filed on it. For almost an hour he worked on the key, inserting it, removing it, filing, inserting.

In the meantime Emily went downstairs and ate a piece of toast and returned with a tray of mugs and coffee. She and the trooper and Mr. Chamberlain sat on the beds and drank their coffee. Mr. Yost dutifully stood at attention in the closet doorway.

At last the key turned completely and the door swung open, to reveal another door with a combination lock. The locksmith produced a stethoscope through which he listened to the lock as he twisted the dial.

"There it is," he said at last, swinging the door open to reveal a small space with only two things inside. He stepped aside for Mr. Yost.

"Mr. Chamberlain, as co-executors of Peter Darrow's estate, I think we should remove those two items together, or I will remove them and you can watch me. Stand where you can see my hands." Calvin Chamberlain obeyed the older man who took a flat leather box from the safe and opened it so that they could all see the contents.

Nestled in white satin was a gold chain with a sapphire pendant and a pair of matching sapphire earrings.

"Mr. Darrow wrote in his journal that he had put something in the safe for Grace. That's it," said Emily happily. "She would have loved those sapphires."

"We will have them appraised," said Mr. Yost handing the box to the minister. "You carry them and together we will put them in the safe in my bank. Is that acceptable, Miss Emily?"

Emily agreed. Poor Mr. Yost was trying so hard to do everything properly. He then removed papers bound together with a black ribbon. He untied the ribbon. "Looks like a standard deed to me, dated 1919. Do you agree, Mr. Chamberlain?" Mr. Chamberlain agreed. "No additions to it." He scanned it briefly. "Thirty chains along the road, turn west, twenty chains along the stone fence to a stake...um...sixty acres, more or less. Seems perfectly clear to me. You may close the safe."

The locksmith wrote some numbers on a card and closed the inside door. "This is the combination. I'll leave the outside door open and make a key for it from this blank." He handed the card to Mr. Yost and they all went downstairs. The locksmith went directly to his car and drove off. The other three men followed her into the sitting room.

"Mr. Chamberlain told me about the confrontation with the bulldozer," Mr. Yost said. "I'm glad you called him. I understand that the man from the Pittsfield Development Corporation insisted that he had purchased all of the land up to the lane."

"I saw the bill of sale," Calvin Chamberlain spoke up.

"But the signature didn't look like Peter Darrow's to me," said Emily. "It was dated last year, but Peter went on paying taxes on all the land. Mr. Wilson said the tax collector was confused and Mr. Darrow was senile."

"The tax collector is methodical, to say the least, and Mr. Darrow was in complete possession of his faculties the last time I saw him." Mr. Yost was positive.

"Could Mr. Wilson, a member of our church, have sold the land to the development corporation and pocketed the money himself?" Mr. Chamberlain shook his head, disbelieving.

"Which would explain why he was so anxious to get his hands on the deed—to make changes in it. What are you going to do about Wilson?" Mr. Yost asked the trooper.

"I don't think there's much we can do, until we have a chance to investigate this land matter, except charge him with vandalism. We still don't know quite what to do about the dogs. The bullets came from Wilson's gun. We know that."

"What about the dogs?" Mr. Yost asked. "I missed them when we drove up."

"They were both shot dead on this property on Saturday afternoon," the trooper explained. "Wilson apparently thought he had to dispose of them so he could get into the house when Miss Emily was away."

Mr. Yost took Emily's hand in his and looked down at her over the top of his half-glasses. "I am grieved for you," he said, and Emily knew that he meant it.

Before the men left, they agreed that they would all meet with the town justice and with Mr. Wilson and anyone else concerned at nine the following morning.

Chapter Twelve

As soon as the banker and the trooper left, Emily ran across the lane. The path through the woods was clearly visible in the daylight. Her ankle hurt but her light heart lifted her over the rough path. Just out of sight of the camp, she began to call to Keith, eager to see him, to run to his arms.

At the last turn she stopped dead. Keith, who had to have heard her calls, was carrying his typewriter to the half-loaded truck. The stakes had been loosened around the tent.

"What are you doing?" Alarmed, she ran to him and took his arm in both of her hands, pressing herself close to him.

He eased her aside with his elbow. "I'm moving out, as you can see."

"Why?"

Carefully he placed the typewriter in the truck. Then he turned and looked at her. "The summer is over. In case you've forgotten, this is Labor Day. I'm going to my home in Williamstown where I'll unload my gear and return the truck. It belongs to the college. I'll pick up my car and tomorrow morning I'll drive to Eugene, Oregon."

"Oregon!" she wailed. "I thought you taught at Williams."

"I do. I'm taking a semester off to teach in Eugene and help plan a wildlife preserve. Fortunately, these arrangements were made almost a year ago."

"Fortunately? What's fortunate about that?"

He smiled at her wryly and her heart did a strange acrobatic maneuver while her knees all but buckled under her.

"Good-by, Emily. I'm glad everything is working out well for you. I assume you found the deed and that it's what you expected."

"Yes, we found the deed. We're going to meet with the justice-of-the-peace tomorrow. You should be there."

"I won't be needed. You can take care of yourself. Please go now and let me get on with my packing."

She stared at him, bewildered, hurt. "But Keith..."

"Go. Oh, and thanks for letting me finish my work with the beavers." He turned and went inside his sagging tent.

She stumbled up the path toward her house where she took care of the puppies, locked the house, and walked off toward the gallery in a trance, forbidding herself to think, trying not to cry. Left foot forward, right foot forward, left, right, left, right.

The weather having improved, there were more customers in the gallery than there had been on the previous days. Emily went right to work, concentrating furiously on woodblock prints and silk screens.

An hour later the door opened and Keith walked in. She looked up expectantly, but he stepped around her without a word and went directly to Nika.

"Came out well," Nika said. "Wait till you see it."

"Just wrap it up. I'll look at it later." He took out his checkbook while Nika went in the back and returned with a wrapped package, which she exchanged for the check.

"Aren't you going to show it to Emily?" Nika asked.

"No." He walked out.

Emily stood like a pillar in the middle of the gallery.

Nika ran to the window. "His truck is loaded. He's leaving. I wonder where he's going."

"To Oregon," Emily said flatly.

Nika beckoned her to the back room. "I don't know what's going on here," Nika said. "Do you know what Dr. Cavanaugh picked up?"

Emily shook her head.

"Pen-and-ink sketches of you. Remember when I sketched you with Job on your steps? That was a commission from Keith Cavanaugh. I showed him the roughs and he was delighted and asked me to do finished drawings—a three-head composite, matted and framed. I asked a handsome price and was almost embarrassed when he agreed to it without a quibble. So why is he going to Oregon without speaking to you? I hear there was some excitement at your place last night. I also heard that the professor was there. This town has ears. Did you fight?"

Emily shook her head.

"Do you want him to go to Oregon?" Nika asked peering into Emily's downcast face.

Again Emily shook her head.

"Do you want to talk about it?" Receiving no answer, Nika picked up the painting of Grace and handed it to her. "Go home," she commanded. "And take curlylocks with you. Decide what it is you want."

"But he has already driven away."

"Go. Remember that Florida is still open, but if you want something else…"

Nika was the second person that day who had ordered Emily to go. She went. She thought until the threads of her thoughts were tangled into a tight mass. At home she sat on her verandah gazing at the portrait of Grace and trying to unravel her thoughts.

Last night Keith had loved her. She could feel his hands as he dried her hair. She could hear his voice as he told her how pretty she was. A long time ago he had commissioned Nika to draw her portrait. He must have loved her then too. So what had happened this morning?

She thought about his first wife who had run off with the author. Passive, Betz had called her. Women were supposed to be passive; that was Grandma Grace's creed. But she was Emily and she knew what she wanted. She wanted Dr. Keith Cavanaugh to come to her and beg her to let him be her master. No she didn't. He'd already had a wife who let one man and then another take care of her. Keith needed a partner.

Yet it was when she was the weakest that he seemed to love her the most, when she needed him to deliver the pups, to protect her from Wilson. Was he disappointed because she didn't have nightmares last night? Is that what went wrong? If she'd known, she could have faked a nightmare, crying out so that he would have come and held her and soothed her. That thought brought her to her feet. She didn't want a phony relationship. She wanted a husband, not a keeper.

She phoned Tommy and asked him to come over right away. Then she dressed carefully in the navy blue dress and heels she had worn to Peter's funeral. When Tommy arrived she gave him a key to her house and instructions about the pups. She told him she'd definitely be back during the night because she had a meeting tomorrow morning, and then she got in her car.

She studied the map and then drove at five miles above the speed limit all the way to Williamstown. It was late afternoon when she arrived, and her confidence was fading with the sun. At the outskirts of town she drew over to the side of the road.

"You can't do this."

"I have to do it. I may fail but at least I can go into old age knowing that I gave it the best I had."

"Ladies do not make advances."

"Shut up, Grace. I don't want a life like yours."

"I had it easy and I was loved and cared for all my life. What's so great about the bruises of the real world? Look at your ankle. That's real enough. Hurts, doesn't it?"

"It hurts a lot after this drive. So does my heart."

"He'll turn you down and then you'll hurt even more. Save yourself. Turn the car around and go home. You have a house, a job in Florida. There will be other men. You look just like me. All you have to do is smile and speak softly, and there will be someone to take care of you. Go back."

"I am not Grace Gresham Potter. I am Emily Stanoszek. My father and mother went on peace marches. I wonder if they ever faced a bulldozer. I can sell art. I can run a guest house. I know what I want. I want to be the wife of Dr. Keith Cavanaugh."

Before the part of her that was Grace had a chance to answer, she gunned her motor and drove into Williamstown where she stopped at a drugstore, checked the phone book, and asked for directions. Then she drove directly to a large frame house. She stopped at the curb, jumped out of the car without allowing herself a moment to primp—or to think—walked purposefully up the walk, and rang the door bell.

She waited, hearing footsteps on stairs, Keith's footsteps. The closer they came, the harder her heart beat and the more her stomach churned. *Dear God,* she prayed, *Help me to...* The door opened.

"Em!" Keith smiled warmly. Then he squared his shoulders and adopted his severe voice. "You wanted something, Emily?"

"I want you." Shocked at her words, she clamped her hand over her mouth.

He laughed and drew her inside and without a word led her up a flight of stairs into a room that was a jumble of papers, stacks of clothing, and half-packed boxes and bags. He closed the door behind them and

179

reached out with both hands, pulling her slowly toward him, devouring her with his eyes.

With the last remnant of her diminishing will, she ducked under his arm and walked across the room. "You sit there," she said pointing to the large chair behind his desk.

"Yes Ma'am," he obeyed.

She wished his eyes would quit twinkling at her. "I will sit here." She sat stiffly on the edge of the couch, staring at the dusty floor. "I wish to speak without interruption until I'm finished. First, I want to tell you about Peter Darrow. I found a journal he wrote while he was building the house. He built it for my grandmother, but she met and married my grandfather. She wrote Peter a letter that he received after her marriage had taken place. He went to Alaska. When he came back fifty years later, he contacted a detective agency in Boston and they sent him a picture of me and said I was the only living descendant of Grace and Thadeus Potter. I look like my grandmother and the picture was with a friend's dog so Peter left the house to me."

"He knew I'd take care of his dogs."

"He was right. You did. Do you like the yellow rose bush?"

"I do. Thank you. Peter knew about Thadeus Potter before the marriage, so he could have gone after Grace, but he didn't. So he's partly to blame if he spent an unhappy life. He didn't do all that he could have done. As for my grandmother, she never did anything but smile prettily and let people take care of her."

"Like Jenny," Keith whispered.

"Betz told me about your wife. I was raised to be like my grandmother. I lost my job in Boston because I was too timid. I was saved from making a decision for myself by the mailgram telling of Peter's death and the house. So I came to Stonefield because I didn't have any place else to go. I stayed because the dogs needed me. I had the backbone of a butterfly."

"Some butterfly. You looked like a tiger attacking that bulldozer," Keith teased.

"Please don't interrupt. I did fix up the house. By the way, how much did you really pay for that chair at the auction?"

"Fifty-five, but I didn't bid against you. I only bid after you had dropped out. You looked so disappointed."

"Thank you. It's a good chair. Back to what I was saying. I found a job and rented rooms and took care of myself. Which brings me to Eddy Riley."

"You don't have to tell me, Em."

"I want to. I did let him help me a lot in my butterfly stage. He's a dear young man. He offered to marry me because he thought I couldn't take care of myself. I refused and quit asking for his help. You obviously didn't know that, or you wouldn't have asked him to come and get me when Job and Bertha were shot."

"No, I didn't."

"You don't know much about me. I'm almost twenty-four. I've never had what people call a love affair. I think—I hope—that you love me. If you do, when you come back from Oregon, you could…"

"Stop, Em." His voice was a command. He got up and came around the desk and sat beside her on the couch, pulling her toward him. "I adore you, Em."

"I don't want to be adored—worshiped, petted. I want to be a partner, an equal. I want to share the good and the not-so-good."

"You upset me, Emily, and you talk too much."

Hurt, she stood up and headed for the door.

"Go sit behind my desk and hear me out," he said. "Turn about is fair play. You upset me because you're so lovely. Sometimes you seem so helpless. When you're helpless, I melt. I'll always remember the two times you ran to me. Both times you could have gone to the Gilberts, but you came to me."

"I could have gone there last night, couldn't I?" She

181

had never even thought of the Gilberts last night.

"But sometimes you are so self-sufficient. You don't need me. You can take care of yourself. And you're so young—you should marry a young man who has never been married before. I'm used merchandise and I'm thirty-one years old."

"So? I just wish I knew what you look like."

He looked surprised. His forehead turned red. He looked down at his jeans and plaid shirt.

"I'm talking about your face," Emily laughed. "What's behind that beard? Not that I really care all that much. You have lovely eyes and the beard makes you look like a beaver, except that you don't have buck teeth."

"I'd do anything for you, love, anything." To her surprise he jumped up from the couch and headed right past her into the hall. "Don't move," he called as he shut a door behind him. She heard water running and splashing. "Shut your eyes and prepare your mind," he called at last. She heard a rustling sound. "Open—and behold!" He was beside her chair, a questioning look on his face.

She stood and reached out to touch his chin. "You have a cleft," she whispered with delight. "The most beautiful cleft I have ever seen."

They wrapped their arms around one another and just stood together in silence for a long time. Then she raised her face and he kissed her tenderly, lovingly.

"Will you marry me?" he whispered.

"I will."

"When? Tomorrow? We could drive to Oregon together."

"I have to be in Stonefield tomorrow, and I can't go anywhere until the pups are taken care of and the estate is settled."

They began to make plans. He could fly back over the long weekend in October. Could she have the dogs taken care of by then? They could return to Oregon after the wedding. Perhaps they could board Bill—and Kezia—with the Gilberts until they returned to Stonefield. Would she want his family to come to the wedding?

"Do you have a mother and father?" she asked.

He studied her, his face pensive. "Yes," he said, "I have a very motherly mother who will be happy to be your mother too. She's always wanted a daughter. Somehow she and Jenny never hit it off. I also have a father and a pair of twin brothers."

"Twins! How old are they?"

"Nineteen."

"Identical?"

"No, thank goodness. John's at Yale. He'll come to the wedding. Jim's at the University of Arizona so you won't get to meet him until Christmas."

"Twins," Emily sighed. "Does that mean we could have twins? Wouldn't that be wonderful? Babies born together would never be alone. No matter what happened they'd always have one another."

"Em!" There was a catch in his voice and moisture in his eyes.

She traced the cleft in his chin with her finger, then wiped the corners of his eyes. "Don't feel sorry for me. I'll never be lonely, not even with you in Oregon, because I'll know you're coming back to me."

"I wasn't feeling so much sorry for you as I was feeling glad for me. You really want to have babies?"

"Definitely—singles, twins, a whole litter."

He held her close. Eventually he took her out to dinner—she had no idea what she ate.

At dawn she was driving back to Stonefield—with Keith in his car right behind her. She thought about Peter Darrow.

Did you see what I did Peter? I went after my man. He wasn't hard to catch. Did you foresee this? I think it's what you would have wanted. You liked him. You wouldn't have wanted him to go on mourning his first love forever—as you did. You know we'll keep on paying the beavers' taxes. There will be little boys to slide down your banister—though I do think that's dangerous.

Keith took care of the pups while she took a shower and then prepared breakfast. After their lingering celebration dinner they had worked all night to finish packing Keith's things. She hadn't slept at all but she felt wide awake, tingling with joy. They walked hand in hand to the town hall and arrived just at nine o'clock.

"Courage," said Keith, kissing her lightly on the cheek as she went forward to sit in a chair held for her by Mr. Yost and Reverend Chamberlain.

She looked back to find Keith, who smiled at her. The room was full. Eddy and Mr. Riley were there, Gil and Ruth Gilbert, the man from the Pittsfield Development Corporation, J. Simon LaRoux, and the trooper who had arrested Wilbert Wilson. The woman named Geraldine sat next to Wilson, who had aged a thousand years in two days, even though his blue-vested suit was immaculate and his long hair was once again carefully arranged to cover his balding head.

A man in baggy pants, open shirt, and a wrinkled jacket came in and took his seat at the desk. The justice-of-the-peace, Mr. Yost said. The justice announced that this was just an informal fact-finding meeting and that they would begin with a report from James Yost, co-executor of the estate of Peter Darrow. One by one they told their stories: Mr. Yost, Eddy Riley, the trooper, and Keith.

Then it was time for the man from the Pittsfield Development Corporation. He testified angrily that he had bought thirty-five acres of land, including the beaver pond, paying fifty thousand dollars to Wilbert Wilson, who said he was acting on behalf of Peter Darrow. He had a bill of sale.

"But you never had a deed," said the justice. "I have seen the deed, talked with the tax collector, examined Peter Darrow's bank account. There is no evidence that he ever saw a penny of that money or signed any document. He paid taxes on the land after the sale was supposed to have been made. If you think you've been cheated, it is up to you to bring whatever action you deem appropriate against Wilbert Wilson. I have no jurisdiction over that." The justice called on the trooper.

"On the night before last, Sunday, we received a call from Dr. Keith Cavanaugh asking us to come to the Peter Darrow house which is now occupied by his heir, Miss Emily Stanoszek. When we arrived we found Wilbert Wilson sitting on the bottom step in the hall. He said Miss Stanoszek had hit him with a hammer. We found that paneling in one of the upstairs bedrooms had been—" The evidence continued.

Finally, the justice announced that there would be a further investigation. He instructed Wilbert Wilson not to leave town in the meantime.

Mr. Yost invited Emily to meet with him and Reverend Chamberlain in his office at the bank. Emily introduced the two executors to her fiancé and Keith was invited to come along.

In his office Mr. Yost said that the estate would be settled in a few days. In addition to the house and sixty acres, and the sapphire jewelry, she would receive approximately seven thousand dollars.

"Trousseau money," said Keith.

"Insulation money," said Emily.

The banker went into a boring, detailed accounting of every penny in the estate.

Then it was Keith's turn. "You've taken good care of Emily," he said. "We appreciate that. I'm leaving for Oregon this afternoon, but I'll be back for the wedding in October. I hope you and Mrs. Yost will attend." Then he turned to the minister. "Emily says that

Wilson tried to bribe you with a promise to remodel the parsonage kitchen. I want to start the kitchen fund." He handed Reverend Chamberlain a check.

Emily, who was taken by surprise, jumped up and kissed Keith on the cheek.

Mr. Yost rose. "Thank you, Dr. Cavanaugh. I will be pleased to attend your wedding. Allow me to say that I think you have chosen a remarkable young woman. Not only is Miss Emily beautiful, I have found her to be very sensible."

"Oh, he didn't choose me. I chose him." Emily laughed as they walked out of the office together.

As they walked home, Emily told Keith about Riley's suggestions for winterizing the sitting-room, kitchen, and bedroom and the rooms above them. Then she took him upstairs and showed him the room over the sitting room.

"Our bedroom," he said with delight. He examined the two back rooms. "Let's put a new bathroom in here over your little bathroom—with a man-sized tub. Bathroom, office and nursery. Perfect."

"I don't go up to the third level," Emily said. "It's full of bats. But we could put in more rooms up there. Go up and see the tower room."

Keith ran up the stairs. "Why don't you have Riley seal the bats out?" he shouted back to her.

"They eat mosquitoes."

"Maybe I like bats after all," he said when he returned. "Now that I'm through with my beaver study, maybe I'll take up bats. In the meantime, why don't we just suggest that they take up residence in the loft over the garage. Hear me?" He shouted up the stairway. "Move to the garage. That's an order. We're going to fill this house ourselves." Then turning to Emily he asked, "Anything else we need to discuss before I leave?"

Emily did have one worry that had been nagging her. She hesitated. "I'd like to continue to rent out rooms to the summer people...ah, maybe...maybe even fix up more rooms on the third floor. And I want to go on working at the gallery with Nika..."

"Perfect!" He gave her a giant bear hug. "I don't teach in the summer. I'll be the house-husband and litter-tender while you do your thing. Come September, we'll reverse roles." He took her chin in his hand and looked deeply into her eyes. "I agree with you, my darling. I want us to be full and equal partners." He kissed her, pressing her body to his.

"I better go," he said huskily.

The Berkshire Hills were ablaze with color on the Friday in October that Keith and his father flew into Albany and his brother drove up from New Haven. Emily went to meet the plane. His mother, Barbara Cavanaugh, who had arrived the week earlier with Keith's grandmother's wedding dress, cooked dinner.

It rained the next morning. Then, just as the guests were assembling in the hall, the sun came out and streamed through the stained-glass window. Mrs. Chamberlain played a lovely song on her guitar as Emily came out of the bedroom over the library and started down the stairs.

The guests gasped as she crossed the landing in the old-fashioned organdy wedding dress. The sun turned her hair, adorned only with a sprig of baby's breath, to a golden halo.

"If she doesn't look like her grandmother," Nika whispered to Josie, nodding toward the portrait of Grace hung between the parlor and library doors.

"Emily has more character." Josie dabbed at her eyes with a handkerchief.

Emily continued down the stairs, gazing deep into Keith's eyes as he waited for her in front of a bank of flowers at the bottom of the steps.

"Dearly beloved, we are gathered here in the sight of God and these witnesses..." The young minister performed the brief ceremony with dignity.

Ruth Gilbert set out an elegant luncheon in Emily's sitting room. One of the girls who helped her serve was leggy with short chestnut-brown hair. Emily watched with pleasure as Eddy helped her load a tray and carried it to the kitchen for her.

The three Cavanaughs drove to New Haven to spend the night with John, assuring her that they could hardly wait to welcome her in their home at Christmas.

When the last guest had left, Keith carried Emily up the stairs, past the stained-glass window, to the bedroom. The antiqued furniture which Emily had moved from the octagonal bedroom was almost hidden by the flowers someone had moved from the downstairs hall. They stood in the bay window looking out over the beaver pond to the gold and crimson hills beyond.

"I promise you, Doctor Keith Cavanaugh," said Emily seriously, "there will be only one man in my life as long as I live." She traced the cleft in his chin with the finger that held her shiny gold band. Then she removed her sapphire earrings and placed them on the dressing table.

Promise Romances® are available at your local book-store or may be ordered directly from the publisher by sending $2.25 plus 75¢ (postage and handling) to the publisher for each book ordered.

If you are interested in joining Promise Romance® Home Subscription Service, please check the appropriate box on the order form. We will be glad to send you more information and a copy of *The Love Letter*, the Promise Romance® newsletter.

Send to: Etta Wilson
Thomas Nelson Publishers
P.O. Box 141000
Nashville, TN 37214-1000

☐ Yes! Please send me the Promise Romance titles I have checked on the back of this page.

I have enclosed _____ to cover the cost of the books ($2.25 each) ordered and 75¢ for postage and handling. Send check or money order. Allow four weeks for delivery.

☐ Yes! I am interested in learning more about the Promise Romance® Home Subscription Service. Please send me more information and a *free* copy of *The Love Letter*.

Name _____

Address _____

City _____ State _____ Zip _____
Tennessee, California, and New York residents, please add applicable sales tax.

OTHER PROMISE ROMANCES®
YOU WILL ENJOY

$2.25 each

☐ 1. IRISH LACE
   Patricia Dunaway

☐ 2. THE CHALLENGED HEART
   Anna Lloyd Staton

☐ 3. A CHANGE OF HEART
   Irene Brand

☐ 4. LOVE TAKES FLIGHT
   Jane Peart

☐ 5. THE HEART OF THE STORM
   Marilyn Young

☐ 6. SONG OF TANNEHILL
   Shirley Sanders

☐ 7. LESSONS IN LOVE
   Patricia Dunaway

☐ 8. TAKEN BY STORM
   Yvonne Lehman

☐ 9. WINDSONG
   Elee Landress

☐ 10. FOR THE LOVE OF ROSES
   Donna Winters

☐ 11. SIGN OF THE CAROUSEL
   Jane Peart

☐ 12. RAINBOW OF PROMISE
   Adell Harvey

☐ 13. IN NAME ONLY
   Irene Hannon

☐ 14. A SONG IN MY HEART
   Constance Robinson

☐ 15. SCENT OF HEATHER
   Jane Peart

☐ 16. A DISTANT CALL
   Patricia Dunaway

☐ 17. MORNING'S SONG
   Suzanna Roberts

☐ 18. PORTRAIT OF LOVE
   Irene Hannon

☐ 19. BRIDGE TO LOVE
   Fran Priddy

☐ 20. LOVE'S DESIGN
   Elee Landress

☐ 21. HONORABLE INTENTIO
   Susan Phillips

☐ 22. ANGELS' TEARS
   Suzanne Roberts

☐ 23. IMPERFECT STRANGER
   Carrole Lerner

☐ 24. A MIGHTY FLAME
   Irene Brand

☐ 25. AUTUMN ENCORE
   Jane Peart

☐ 26. TUESDAY'S CHILD
   LouAnn Gaeddert

Dear Reader:

I am committed to bringing you the kind of romantic novels you want to read. Please fill out the brief questionnaire below so we will know what you like most in Promise Romances®.

Mail to: Etta Wilson
Thomas Nelson Publishers
P.O. Box 141000
Nashville, Tenn. 37214-1000

1. Why did you buy this Promise Romance®?

☐ Author
☐ Back cover description
☐ Christian story
☐ Cover art
☐ Recommendation
from others
☐ Title
☐ Other_____

2. What did you like best about this book?

☐ Heroine
☐ Hero
☐ Christian elements
☐ Setting
☐ Story line
☐ Secondary characters

3. Where did you buy this book?

☐ Christian bookstore
☐ Supermarket
☐ Drugstore
☐ General bookstore
☐ Home subscription
☐ Other (specify)_____

4. Are you interested in buying other Promise Romances®?

☐ Very interested   ☐ Somewhat interested
                    ☐ Not interested

5. Please indicate your age group.
   ☐ Under 18   ☐ 25-34
   ☐ 18-24   ☐ 35-49   ☐ Over 50

6. Comments or suggestions?

7. Would you like to receive a free copy of the Promise Romance® newsletter? If so, please fill in your name and address.

Name _____

Address _____

City _____ State _____ Zip _____

7375-7